Coming Around Again

Sydney Campbell

Coming Around Again

ISBN: 978-1-990231-22-3

Cover design by abu-chan
Editing by Megan Records

For HB - let's see how far we can take this.

Other books by Sydney Campbell:

Temptation - An Allie Styles Romance (Book 1)
Deception - An Allie Styles Romance (Book 2)
Reckonings - An Allie Styles Romance (Book 3)
Beginnings - An Allie Styles Romance (Book 4)

The Allie Styles Romance Boxed Set

Reawakening - Courtyard Tales of
Contemporary Romance (Book 1)
Redemption - Courtyard Tales of Contemporary
Romance (Book 2)
Reckless - Courtyard Tales of Contemporary
Romance (Book 3)

Acting out of Love - Mountain Valley Romance
(Book 1)
No Reservations Required - Mountain Valley
Romance (Book 2)
A Dash of Romance - Mountain Valley
Romance (Book 3)
Coming Around Again - Mountain Valley
Romance (Book 4)
Last Call - Mountain Valley Romance (Book 5)

CHAPTER ONE

Lainey

"Ladies and gentlemen, we're now approaching Mountain Valley, the end of the line. Please ensure you have your personal belongings with you. Your luggage will be retrieved from underneath the bus once we arrive at the terminal. As you'll have noticed, there's a storm coming and caution is urged for the rest of your travels this evening. Thanks for riding with Great Lines."

I looked up from my screen for the first time in God knows how long and peered out the window. The snow was indeed coming down. I should've hired a car, but the last thing I'd wanted was to return here looking all uppity.

I could barely see the mountains that I knew surrounded us. It had been over a decade since

I'd been home, but some things you never forget. I shut my laptop in frustration. Aside from serving as a distraction from the storm, my attempt at writing on the trip had been laughable. I tried not to think about my looming deadline, but it was impossible. It was like the devil on my shoulder, taunting me.

I packed everything up and was pulling on my coat when my cell phone started buzzing. I searched my purse until I found it, dismayed to see I was on the last bar. I'd have to charge it in the rental car on the drive. I saw who was calling and grimaced. The devil on my other shoulder.

"Hey," I said.

"Hello there," Beth, my agent, said. "Have you arrived?"

"I have, but I also have no battery left on my phone, so I may cut out on you. I'll get back in touch when I'm charged."

"Already making excuses, are you? You need to finish this script, Elena. You know that. They start pre-production in a month. They're already thinking about casting."

"I know, I know. I'm on it."

"I'm still not sure why you had to actually go there to write the damn thing," Beth continued, almost to herself.

"I told you. I haven't been home since my

mom died. This film is about family relationships. When you throw in the fact that Mason Scott's studio, which is right here, is producing it, it just makes sense, don't you think?"

"If you say so."

The bus slowed to a halt and I stood, gathering my purse and backpack.

"Listen, Beth, I've got to go. The bus just pulled in and the snow is fierce. I'll speak to you soon."

"You be careful. Death will not be a valid excuse for missing this deadline."

I laughed as I hung up the phone and dropped it back in my purse. But when I set foot in the parking lot, I wasn't laughing anymore. At some point between me glancing out the window and stepping off the bus, the storm had really picked up. I pulled up my hood and quickly retrieved my luggage before heading over to the rental car kiosk. I'd lived in these mountains until I was eighteen years old. I knew them like the back of my hand.

The "bus terminal" was really nothing more than the parking lot of the one tiny strip mall in the village. My last visit had been right after my twenty-fifth birthday, ten years earlier, to bury my mother. I was already living in LA at that point, and after her death there was no reason to come back. Until now.

As I walked towards the kiosk, I noticed a couple of new storefronts, and one new café, but the rest was like it was stuck in a time capsule. I shook my head and approached the door. It was closed. There was a sign that read, *Closed due to storm. For emergencies, call 555-385-5555.*

I pulled my phone out of my purse, but the battery was dead. *Shit.* I looked around, but all the windows were dark, save one. I tucked my phone away, pulled my hood further up over my head, and walked towards the door. I tried it, and mercifully it was open. I walked inside and pulled off my hood, shaking the light dusting of snow from my hair. It was only then that I stopped to take a good look around.

The shop was narrow and lit by a string of fairy lights on either side of the ceiling. It was more of a workshop than a store, with gorgeous wood furniture packed into the space. Dressers, coffee tables, bookshelves—all beautifully carved wood. Works of art, really. I took my time, looking around and running the tips of my near-frozen fingers over the table tops. There was a distinctive quality to the furniture that appealed to me. It was warm and it felt like it was almost made just for me. There wasn't a piece in the place that I didn't love.

I looked towards the back of the shop but there was no one there. There was a closed door, leading either to a staircase, a backroom, or a washroom for all I knew. I figured whoever owned the place would show up eventually. There was no reason they wouldn't let me use a phone to call for a car. I walked back to the front of the shop, looking out the large picture window at the snow swirling around outside. It was getting thicker and I worried the longer I waited, the tougher the drive was going to be and it was already dark. I checked my phone for the time, momentarily forgetting the dead battery was the reason I was standing there. I figured it had to be at least seven-thirty.

I gazed out the window, mesmerized by the beauty of the mountains I couldn't even see. I must have been lost in space because I didn't notice the back door open or close before I heard someone clear their throat.

"Can I help you? I was just about to close up," a deep male voice asked.

I turned around to ask about the phone when my heart stopped. At least, it must have stopped. There was no other explanation for the fact that I could no longer breathe, see straight, or even form a coherent thought. I tried to swallow but there was nothing doing.

For a moment, I honestly thought I was going to pass out, because standing there, about ten feet away, was Logan Matthews, my high school boyfriend.

Taller than I remembered, he'd filled out in the years since I'd seen him. Broad shoulders, defined muscles, and a mop of curly brown hair that fell over his face. My only serious boyfriend, the one who ruined me for any other man. And I hadn't seen him in seventeen years, unless you count our non-exchange at my mother's funeral a decade ago.

"Lainey."

I finally swallowed.

"Elena," I corrected.

He laughed, hesitantly walking closer.

"That's right. Elena Wise, Hollywood screenwriter." He smiled, coming to stop about two feet away.

"Logan."

"Lainey."

We stood there for an eternity, or maybe 30 seconds, just staring into each other's eyes. Everything I'd accomplished since high school melted away and I was 18 years old again, graduating and looking forward to college and life outside of a small town. My friends were all taking off in different directions, there was nothing keeping me there—except Logan.

"This is all yours?" I asked, gesturing to the furniture.

"Yeah." He gave a soft laugh. "I guess woodworking kind of stuck."

I looked around in amazement.

"I'd say so. What the hell are you still doing in this shit town?"

He took a deep breath and let it out slowly before replying. I saw all the emotions I'd felt a moment earlier pass through his eyes.

"Are we going to start already?"

"Sorry," I said, shaking my head.

He took another step closer and reached out, letting his hand hover in the air between us.

"Can I —" he asked.

I nodded and before I knew it, he had me wrapped up in his arms. I stood there, just absorbing the moment, before I let my arms find their way around his familiar shape. I rested my cheek against his chest as he stroked my hair. I had come in looking to make a phone call. I was beyond confused. I pulled away and looked up at him.

"Seriously, Logan. I can't believe you're still here. How are your parents?"

"My dad passed away. My mom's okay. Getting older. I moved her to a retirement home in the city. But what...what are you doing here?"

He looked out the front window, confused.

"There's a storm, you know?" he said.

"Thanks, Captain Obvious. I rented a cottage for a few weeks. I'm on deadline for my next project, and, well, fuck it, I've got writer's block. The film is about complicated family relationships and takes place in a small mountain town, so coming home made sense."

I stopped talking long enough to notice he wasn't looking at my face but at my left hand. I covered it immediately with my right and glanced at his hands, both of which were bare. I nervously twisted the band around my ring finger, the feeling so foreign to me.

"It's not what you think, Logan—"

"What do I think? That you got married? I knew you'd get married, Lainey."

"I'm not. I'm not married. And I'm not Lainey anymore. Elena. I told you."

Logan shook his head.

"Sorry. You'll always be Lainey to me." He studied me for a heartbeat. "What do you mean, you're not married?"

"I'm not. It's an inside joke. My agent, Beth, made me wear it while I was here so I wouldn't get hit on. She's very focused on me finishing."

"Hit on? In a cabin in the mountains?"

"She's a lady living in LA. She doesn't

understand cottage life. Or isolation of any sort, for that matter. Anyway, I would love to catch up, but the reason I came in was that the rental car place is closed and I need a car to get up to the cabin. Have you got a phone I can use?"

Logan smiled his old easy smile and once again time evaporated. It took all my energy to focus. After the plane trip and the bus ride and the building storm—it was all a bit much.

"I'll drive you," he said. "Len's not going to open the rental shop now. The roads are too bad. Let's get your stuff."

"You sure?"

"Positive. It'll give us a chance to catch up."

I smiled and waited for him to lock up. When he was done, he grabbed my bags and took me out to his truck. He loaded everything into the back and we climbed into the cab. He reached over and gave my hand a quick squeeze before starting the engine. I turned on the radio, flipping through the stations until I landed on Dobie Gray singing *Drift Away*. I settled back into my seat and looked out the passenger window, watching the trees go by in the dark, almost hidden behind a veil of snow.

"Where's the cottage?" Logan asked.

"Just off Route 6."

"Bear Lake?"

I nodded. He sighed.

"Nice choice. Quiet."

"That's the plan. I need quiet to write."

"Well, unfortunately, I don't think we're going to make it there tonight."

I looked over at him.

"What do you mean?"

"They closed that road half an hour ago. No way in or out."

"Shit. I'm sure we'll manage. Can we try?"

"You got groceries? A cord of wood? Have you even got toilet paper?"

I stared ahead through the windshield, not bothering to answer.

"I didn't think so," he said. "Listen. I'm doing some renovation work at a B&B just off the next road. They owe me a favour. I'm sure they'll find room for you."

"Logan. I need to get to my cottage."

"Well, you're not getting there tonight. It's too dangerous. Too much of a risk."

I bit my tongue. Once again, that decade disappeared, but this time not in a good way. This was always our problem—I was ready to forge ahead, he was too scared to take risks. That's how I ended up leaving this shit hole while he stayed.

But in this case, I had to admit he was right. I wasn't equipped to ride out a mountain storm. If there was no power, I wouldn't even have a phone, forget transportation.

"Fine. Take me to the B&B."

We drove without speaking as the snow came down around us. I honestly had no idea how Logan was able to navigate. If that was the prize for staying, I was glad I'd gotten out. After a few minutes, he pulled onto a small gravel road and stopped in front of a large rambling house. We got out and he grabbed my bags. Neither of us said a word as we walked up the steps and went inside.

CHAPTER TWO
Lainey

Logan held the door open and I heard the jingle of the overhead bell. Despite my annoyance at the situation, I had to smile. It was just so *quaint*. I made a mental note to include that in the film somewhere.

We walked over to the front desk and a gentleman in his seventies came out of what I assumed to be the office door. He was well put together, with sandy hair and blue eyes that crinkled at the corner. You could tell he'd been a looker in his day. He was dressed impeccably in a cable-knit sweater and jeans. A smile lit up his face when he saw Logan.

"Logan! What a surprise. You do realize there's a storm outside, right?"

Logan laughed.

15

"That's why I'm here, Grant. Small emergency. My friend, Lainey—"

"Elena," I interrupted. Logan shot me a look before continuing.

"...rented a cabin, but the roads are closed. I was hoping you'd have a room for her?"

"Absolutely. All our guests canceled—" Grant gestures vaguely towards the storm. "We've got plenty of room. In fact, I'll make one up for you, too."

Logan shook his head.

"No need. I'll be on my way."

I turned to look outside, chewing the inside of my lip while contemplating my next move.

"I thought it was too dangerous to drive any further," I ventured.

Logan shot me a dirty look, but Grant smiled. As we stood there in a stand-off, a woman emerged from the back room. Also in her seventies, she had grey hair tied up in a loose bun, a few strands framing her face. She was similarly dressed in a sweater and jeans and walked over to join Grant.

"Hi, Logan. What brings you here tonight?"

Grant turned to her, putting his arm over her shoulder.

"Sadie, Logan and his friend, Elena, will be staying with us until the storm passes. Seems they got stuck out on the roads, trying to get to

Elena's cabin."

Sadie smiled warmly and nodded.

"Lovely," she said. "I'll get dinner started."

*

We took the stairs together, Logan still carrying my bags. He led the way down the hall, which was clearly under renovation. There were a lot of exposed beams and plaster work left to be done.

"Don't mind the state of disarray. I've been working on the place forever. It's always one thing or another."

He opened the first door on the right. We walked in and I noticed was the beautifully carved headboard and the stately mahogany dresser. The walls, however, needed a paint job and the fixtures needed updating. I smiled to myself.

"Furniture looks familiar," I said.

"Well, I produce a ridiculous amount of it and I don't have a lot of storage space—"

"So you let it go for half its worth?"

Logan blushed.

"I'm sorry. I just can't help but feel you're undervaluing your work. Do you even have a website set up to sell to people in the city?"

Logan smiled and backed out of the room.

"I'll see you at dinner, Lainey."

He shut the door and I sat down on the bed. There was no point in unpacking. I planned to leave as soon as the roads cleared. I kicked off my shoes and laid down, closing my eyes and enjoying the silence. I must have dozed off because before I knew it, I heard the dinner bell ring.

*

Dinner was lovely. We ate in the kitchen, which at first I found a little odd until Grant explained that Logan was renovating the dining room. It was just the four of us and the food was delicious. The three of them chatted non-stop while I took in the surroundings. It was a beautiful kitchen—country-style but with state-of-the-art equipment. There was a long gas range and a commercial-size fridge, both in stainless steel. The walls were sparkling white—not a trace of grease to be seen. I was impressed.

"Isn't that true, Lainey?" Logan said.

I shook myself out of my reverie and turned my attention back to my dinner companions. All three sets of eyes were staring at me expectantly. I smiled sheepishly.

"I'm sorry. I wandered off for a moment. Isn't what true?"

"That you're here to finish your latest movie."

I cleared my throat and put down my fork.

"In theory, yes. I actually grew up here," I said, glancing over at Grant and Sadie.

Sadie looked delighted.

"Did you? Well, isn't that lovely. Is that how the two of you know each other?"

Logan and I exchanged a quick grin.

"You could say that. I moved away after high school. We haven't seen each other in years," I said, then changed the subject. "Did the two of you buy this place recently? I remember it being run by the Howes."

Logan looked over, impressed.

"Good memory, Lainey. Yeah, the Andersons took over about eight years ago, right?"

Grant nodded happily, spearing another piece of meat with his fork. I turned to Logan.

"Where are you living these days?" I asked.

The room fell silent and Logan busied himself with his food for a moment before clearing his throat.

"Actually, I bought your mom's place."

I stared at him, blinking. How did I not

know this? When I'd last come, I'd stayed for a while to settle the estate, and I'd opted to put the house on the market. I hadn't wanted to come back to sign the papers when it sold, so I gave power of attorney to an old friend of my mom's. No one had ever told me who bought the house, and I hadn't even thought to ask. I'd just wanted to put as much distance between Mountain Valley and myself as possible.

Logan had bought my house.

"Oh, Lainey *Wise?* Logan, you didn't mention that." Sadie laughed.

Logan shot her a look and she clammed up, suddenly very interested in the bread basket.

"You're living in my mother's house?" I asked, just to make sure I understood.

"I am. I've been renovating it slowly for years. You should, uh, come by while you're in town. There's actually quite a bit of stuff I've put away for you."

I had completely lost my appetite. My mother's death had been the hardest thing I'd ever had to endure. I'd grown up without a father—it had always been just the two of us, right from the beginning. As a result, we had a very complicated relationship: part close, part co-dependent, part bitter. Since she'd died, I'd buried everything except the fondness.

I was an expert at burying memories, but the

idea that Logan was sitting on a goldmine of my mother's belongings… was a little too much to process at the moment. I pushed back my chair, standing up.

"You know, I think I'm just going to go and lie down. It's been a really long day. Thank you so much, Sadie, Grant, for your hospitality and an excellent dinner. Logan, I'll see you in the morning. Thanks again for coming to my rescue tonight."

CHAPTER THREE

Logan

"I'm not quite sure I handled that in the best possible way," I muttered, standing up to clear my plate.

"You don't say," Grant laughed.

Sadie walked over and put a hand on my shoulder, taking the plate from me.

"I can't believe that's the girl. How on earth —?" she asked.

"She walked off the bus and into my shop, completely out of nowhere. It was like no time had passed and we were eighteen again. Seventeen years, up in smoke. Crazy," I said.

"Maybe it's fate. Sometimes, two people are just meant to be."

I laughed.

"I'd have done anything for Lainey, except

22

the one thing she needed me to do," I said.

"And what's that?" Grant asked.

"Leave Mountain Valley."

He eyed me.

"And now that you've seen her again, was staying worth it?"

I didn't have an answer.

*

I went up to my room after dinner and laid down on the bed, fully clothed, and stared up at the ceiling. The events of the day were finally sinking in. Lainey was here. In this house. In the room right next to mine. I laughed out loud. It was too crazy to be true.

The moment I saw her in my shop, time stopped. She had stood there, barely 5'3", her light brown hair falling just past her shoulders. Her hazel eyes, the ones that had haunted me since high school, were just as fierce and inquisitive as ever. Sure, she had a few years on her since the last time I'd seen her, but hell, so did I. The woodworking kept me fit, but I certainly wasn't the athlete I'd been back in high school.

I knew she was a screenwriter. Everyone knew that. Being from a small town meant that even after you left and tried to forget, everyone back home still cheered on your success, claiming you as their own. We'd all been watching her career grow and thrive for years. I'd never dreamed it might one day bring her back.

I'd seen her briefly at her mom's funeral. I'd wanted nothing more than to take her in my arms and comfort her, but instead, I'd kept my distance, standing in the back and out of sight, not wanting to make the day any more difficult for her.

I hadn't asked how long she was in town for. It didn't seem important. My mind had instantly gone to how I could maximize that time. From the moment we got into my car we were bickering, but fuck it. Seventeen years and I'd never found anyone like Lainey. And I'd tried.

When I saw that ring on her finger, my heart dropped. It felt like a sucker punch that she'd found someone to replace me. The relief that flooded my body when she admitted it was a ruse almost knocked me over. I didn't even know if I still had a chance with her, but I was damn glad she wasn't married.

I rolled over onto my side, thinking about the house. I'd known from the minute I laid eyes on her I'd have to come clean. I'd been turning it over in my head all night, how to best bring it up. Then she went and asked, and I couldn't lie to her.

Several times I'd thought about writing to her, or even calling, just to let her know about the letters and journals I'd found stashed away in the attic. They belonged with her, but I couldn't bring myself to make the call. I knew the moment she collected them, or worse, sent for them, any ties I might have to her would be severed. I'd kept those boxes in my back pocket like a trump card, to be played when the time came.

That time had come.

She was angry with me now, but I knew her well enough to know that anger would die down. I also knew her well enough to know she did not eat enough at dinner. The only reason I hadn't undressed was that I knew, as sure as I knew it was still snowing outside, that within the hour, Lainey would be up and looking for food.

I smiled to myself, reassured that I still knew her, even though we'd just been kids. High school graduates. What did we know about anything? For all my pining, it was possible we weren't even compatible anymore. We may have both grown into completely different individuals. She was a Hollywood screenwriter, for Christ's sake. I highly doubted she'd be content going off for a weekend in the wilderness with nothing but a tent, a knife, and a pack of matches. There was no way she was still the same Lainey.

I rolled over again, once more staring at the ceiling. This constant second-guessing everything was killing me. I wished I had a piece of wood to carve, a surface to sand, something to take my mind off things. I checked my phone. It was almost midnight. Wouldn't be long now.

CHAPTER FOUR
Lainey

I managed to fall asleep but by midnight I was wide awake. I slid out of bed and peered out the window. The snow was still coming down. I couldn't even make out Logan's truck. The area surrounding the B&B was lined by tall evergreen trees, their branches covered in a heavy, white blanket. The moon was hidden behind the clouds but it was almost as light as mid-day, with the snow reflecting off the overcast sky. I don't know how long I stood there watching the flakes drift, but when my stomach growled, I knew it was time to move.

I dug around in my suitcase and fished out my slippers, then padded out into the hallway. I went a few paces and stopped outside Logan's door, tapping softly. I didn't want to wake him, but if he was already up, I was game for a partner in crime.

"What is it, Lainey?" he called.

I opened the door, peering in. He was fully dressed, lying on his bed reading a book. I walked in and saw it was a copy of Ken Grimwood's *Replay*.

"That's a good one," I said.

"Not the first time I've read it. I just found it on the bedside table. In fact, I think it might be a copy I left here." He laughed and set the book aside. "What's up?"

"Hungry," I said. "Want to come explore the kitchen?"

He grinned and swung his legs off the bed, rising to join me.

*

I stood in front of the open fridge, contemplating our options.

"The thing is," I said, "I don't want to screw anything up for us tomorrow. Like, if I eat this cake, does that mean there won't be dessert after lunch? How long do you think this storm will last?"

Logan rolled his eyes at me.

"Shut the fridge door. I've got just the

28

thing."

I did as I was told and hopped up onto the butcher-block counter, letting my legs swing into the empty space beneath. I watched with interest as he grabbed a step-stool and took it over to the corner. He got up, reached into a high cabinet, and came down triumphant, holding a box of cellophane-wrapped chocolates in his hand. I clapped my hands in delight.

"Oh, good show, Logan!"

He walked over and hopped up next to me, unwrapping the box as he settled into a comfortable position. Once it was free of the plastic, I grabbed it from him and tore off the lid. Discarding the map, I plucked out a chocolate and handed him the box. He took it from me, laughing, and waited. I took a bite, wrinkled up my nose, and dropped it back in the box before selecting another.

"You never change, do you? Why can't you just read the map?" he asked.

"That's no fun," I said as I sunk my teeth into a luscious square of thick salted caramel, closing my eyes in ecstasy.

I reached in for another one. Coconut. *Yuck.* I dropped it in the box and found a nut cluster.

"That used to drive me crazy," he confessed. "But now it's kind of funny. Plus, I get to eat all the rejects."

Logan reached into the box and pulled out the coconut monstrosity, popping it in his mouth. I stopped eating and watched him for a moment.

"Why didn't you ever tell me that bothered you?" I asked.

He just shrugged and picked up my first chocolate, dropping it in his mouth and chewing thoughtfully before answering.

"I was never good with conflict. I guess I decided to pick my battles, and that wasn't one of them."

I considered this as I studied the box, settling on a round chocolate. Raspberry. Jackpot. Logan looked on, disappointed.

"Since when do you like the fruit ones?" he asked.

"I grew up. My tastes changed."

I jumped down off the counter and opened the fridge again.

"Milk?" I asked. "Or vodka?"

"Vodka," he answered without hesitation.

I opened the freezer, pulled out the vodka, and grabbed two glasses from the drying rack by the sink. Logan took the bottle from me and unscrewed the top. I held out the glasses and he poured us each a couple of fingers. I raise my glass in salute, and after a brief clink, we both downed our drinks. I immediately felt the alcohol course through my veins. I was warm everywhere, and the world around me took on a slightly fuzzy feel. It had been a long time since I'd had a drink, and I had always been a cheap drunk in the first place. I smiled uncertainly at Logan.

"Still can't hold your alcohol?" he asked, smiling.

"I guess we'll see," I said.

"Come here," he said, reaching out for me.

I walked toward him, and when I was close enough, he reached out and ran his thumb just under my lip, in the indent above my chin. It was an innocent gesture, but it brought back feelings I hadn't had in a long time and suddenly, I was looking at Logan in a different light. He smiled and showed me his thumb, which was covered in caramel. I laughed, and then for some reason (okay, fine, alcohol), I took his thumb and licked the caramel off. His eyes widened, but before I had a chance to register this, he was kissing me.

Logan was kissing me.

My first thought was *when was the last time someone kissed me?* I couldn't remember, and I couldn't understand why. Kissing was really good. I should have definitely been doing it more often. My next thought was *Logan is kissing me!!* I had no idea what to do about that one, so for the moment I just decided to go with it. As soon as he felt me relax, he put his hands on my hips and pulled me towards him, in the space between his legs.

I brought my hands up to his face, feeling the rough stubble of a day's growth on his jawline. He smelled so good. He tasted so good. I closed my eyes and let myself get lost as his hands worked over my back, drawing me still closer until they ended up on the back of my head. I pulled away a little and he wound his fingers through my hair, unwilling to let me go.

"I've been thinking about this since the minute you walked into my shop," he whispered.

I didn't know what to say. Had I? I didn't know. It certainly wasn't forefront in my mind, but it also felt kind of...inevitable?

"We can't do this," I said.

"Why not?"

"Because I came here to write a script, not pick up the threads of a relationship that unraveled seventeen years ago."

He flinched, and I felt a flash of regret. I reached up to stroke his hair but he pulled away. I sighed and backed up. The mood was definitely broken.

"I'm sorry."

"No, it's okay. At least you phrased it poetically."

"Listen, I didn't mean it like that. I just meant that I didn't come here looking for complications. I came here looking for a quiet place to write."

"And it didn't occur to you that we'd see each other?"

"I had no idea you were even still here. We never kept in touch. How was I to know?"

"Whose fault is that?"

"Christ, Logan, I'm not here to start a fight or cast blame. I'm certainly not here to examine the details of where we went wrong. I have enough on my mind right now. I have a movie to write."

"Okay, okay. I'm sorry. I guess this is still a sore spot."

"You don't say."

We were both silent for a few moments, until I couldn't stand it and reached over to pluck a chocolate from the box. He laughed and the ice was broken.

"So tell me," he said. "What's the movie about?"

I jumped back up onto the counter chose another chocolate.

"It's a drama, set in a small town, between an estranged mother and daughter. They come together after years of not speaking at the funeral of their husband/father, whom they both adored. It was a hard story for me to write, and the polish is due in a month when pre-production starts."

"I can imagine that was hard," Logan said quietly.

Logan was one of the few people I'd ever confided in about my father, or rather, my lack of a father. The one topic my mother never discussed. It was like I'd come from thin air. Logan was the only person I'd ever discussed this with, how it made me feel to have either been abandoned or God knew what. To then have to write a film about a close father/daughter relationship in which the mother was on the outside, well—

"Yeah. Talk about bringing baggage into a project. Anyway, given a whole bunch of circumstances, it made sense to come here to finish it up."

"And—" he prodded.

"And it would force me to finally deal with some shit of my own, I guess." I looked at him. "You don't miss a thing, do you?"

"Lainey, I can read you like a book."

I rolled my eyes and hopped off the counter, pulling my phone out of my pajama pants pocket.

"Don't be so smug about it. Tell me about you. What's the name of your company?"

"Logan Designs."

"How original." I scrolled through my phone. "Why don't I see anything online? What's the website address?"

"I don't have a website."

I glanced at him over my phone.

"Instagram?"

"Huh?"

"You're building gorgeous furniture in a fairytale setting and you don't have an Instagram account? What is wrong with you?"

"I'm not into that crap."

I knew that. Countless times I'd tried to find him online.

"You're not into sales," I countered.

I logged into Instagram and created an account for him.

"Unlock your phone and pass it to me," I said.

He gave me a funny look, but he did it. I downloaded the app and when it prompted me for his password, I asked him for it. Again he gave me that look, but he obliged. Then I scrolled through his camera roll and uploaded a few pictures of dressers and tables he had. He sat there studying me with a worried look as I worked. I put in some prices that I thought were reasonable, threw in some hashtags, and tossed the phone back to him. I wasn't worried about him catching it—he'd played football in high school.

"Username is LoganDesigns, one word, and the password is ThunderR0ad, upper case T and R, replace the o with a zero."

He looked at his phone like it was a foreign object.

"And what am I supposed to do with that information?"

"Manage your Instagram account. I uploaded a few of your pieces. You have no e-commerce site set up yet, so you can't actually do any transactions online, but you can add in an email address and people can get in touch that way for now. Just look at what I did and copy it with any piece you want to sell."

Logan was staring at me like I was crazy.

"Find other artisans you like and start following them and liking their stuff. They'll reciprocate once they see how good you are. Best case scenario, you collaborate with someone whose work you really like. Worst case? Nothing. Either way, I guarantee you'll sell some furniture."

He tucked his phone into his back pocket and shook his head as if trying to clear it. I let a small chuckle escape as I watched him.

"You really don't understand any of this, do you?"

He shook his head slowly.

"I don't. I just want to make furniture."

"And sell it to local B&Bs? Come on, you're better than that. You can do more."

He sighed.

"I really don't want to get into this tonight. I've had too much chocolate and vodka."

"Okay. I can respect that. But we're not done here," I said.

He hopped off the counter and put the chocolates away.

"We are for tonight."

He took my hand and led me out of the kitchen. We walked up the stairs and said goodnight outside our bedroom doors. A part of me hoped he was going to kiss me again, but he didn't. He just watched me with a curious expression on his face, one I didn't recognize.

"It's been a really long day—" I started.

He nodded solemnly.

"Sleep well, Lainey."

He smiled and disappeared into his room.

CHAPTER FIVE

Logan

I was up the next morning just after dawn. I spent a while in bed, thinking about the night before, wondering if things might have gone differently. After chasing that thought for a while, I got up, pulled on some clothes, and headed down to the dining room.

Sadie was already up, setting the breakfast table. I said good morning then walked over to the back bay of windows, looking out into the storm that was still swirling around outside. It had been coming down for over 12 hours now, but it was finally slowing down.

"Blessing or a curse?" Sadie asked.

I had to smile.

"I'll let you know," I replied. "Is there anything I can do to help? In the kitchen, or—"

She waved me off with a dismissive gesture.

"Don't be silly. Do you want to wait for Elena to eat?"

"No," I laughed. "Who knows when she'll wake up."

"Excuse me?"

I turned to the voice behind me, and there stood Lainey, fully dressed and made-up like she was heading out shopping.

"What are you doing up? Isn't it like, three o'clock in the morning for you?" I asked.

"Something like that. My schedule is all messed up anyway, so I figured I should just get up and push through for as long as I could." She wandered over towards the kitchen. "What's for breakfast?"

Sadie burst out laughing and walked to the stove, only to return with a plate of steaming cinnamon buns. The moment she set them on the table, Lainey's hand snaked in to grab one.

"Oh my god, these are amazing," she said, devouring the first one before reaching for a second.

"Well, when you get settled, you should head down to Franni's bakery. That's where they're from."

"God, I remember Franni's. Is Mrs. Simon still—"

"No," Sadie said, cutting her off. "She died

quite a few years ago. The place is run by three lovely young people now. In the meantime, maybe slow down, because there's still pancakes, eggs, and bacon coming," Sadie said.

Lainey looked at me, eyebrow raised, a guilty expression on her face.

"I'm being a pig, aren't I?" she asked as Sadie retreated to the stove.

I laughed.

"Not at all. She loves it, trust me. She loves nothing more than to feed people. Just sit down and prepare to gorge."

Lainey whipped out her chair and sat down, snapping her napkin open and spreading it over her lap.

"Ready!"

*

After breakfast, I took Lainey around the big old house, showing her all the work I was doing, the pieces I'd made. She touched everything, commenting on one aspect or another. Every once in a while, she'd snap a picture and upload it to that website she kept going on about. I didn't argue.

We thought about venturing outside but decided against it. The snow had tapered off but the wind was still pretty vicious, and the fire in the sitting area was looking pretty damn inviting. We curled up on either side of the couch and I threw her a blanket. After a few moments, she broke the silence.

"So you're living in my mom's house. That's not weird?"

I knew it was coming. I was just glad she wasn't angry.

"No. I've done a lot of work on the place. And it's not like it was your childhood home. She sold that ages ago. This was just a small cottage, off the back road that cuts through—"

"I know where it is," she said.

"Right. Of course. I'm sorry. I didn't mean to imply—"

"Whatever. Just drop it."

I shut my mouth instead of saying what was really on my mind and let a few minutes pass before venturing back out onto safer ground.

"You should come by and see it sometime. Plus, like I said, I've got that stuff for you. I could also drop it by the place you're renting."

She nodded, deep in thought.

"It's not that I meant to stay away," she murmured, almost to herself. "I wanted to visit her. I just didn't want to come *here*."

"Why?"

She shook her head, clearly unsure.

"I think because this place makes me feel small. As long as I was here, I just wanted to get out. And when I did, when I found my home in LA, I was finally able to breathe. Which sounds ridiculous when you compare this air to that air, but you know what I mean. Metaphorically speaking."

"I do. But I don't understand why. I've always been so happy here."

"Yeah," she said. "I don't get that. You have so much talent—you could be anywhere."

"I'm right where I want to be."

She pushed away the blanket and stood up, walking over to poke at the fire. I left her in silence, letting her work out whatever shit she had to work out in her head. I was content to just be in the same room with her, to be able to watch her, have her so close I could touch her.

"What are you thinking?" she asked.

I smiled.

"Nothing, really. Just about how the storm seems to have eased up."

She nodded.

"I should probably put together a list of stuff I need to get." She wandered over to the desk, where a pad and a mug filled with pens lay.

She sat down on the chair and selected a pen, drawing the pad closer to her. She started scribbling and crossing out, scribbling and crossing out. I crossed the room and put my hand on her wrist, stopping her.

"It's okay. Relax. We'll get you sorted out."

She looked up at me, relief washing over her face. She looked incredibly vulnerable. It wasn't a look I was used to seeing on her. I didn't like it.

"Hey," I said. "What's wrong?"

She shook her head, drawing her hair behind her and tying it up with an elastic she slipped off her wrist.

"I don't know. Just being here is unsettling."

I wasn't sure what to say to that. Eventually, she heaved a heavy sigh and stood up, pushing the pad aside.

"I've got an idea," I said. "Follow me."

*

I led Lainey into the kitchen, where we found the Andersons pulling out the fixings for lunch.

"Don't bother," I said. "I'm going to take Lainey on a picnic."

Grant turned to look at me, smiling, and handed me a fresh baguette.

"Straight from the oven," he said.

I grabbed it and handed it to Lainey, who took it with a laugh.

43

"A picnic? Where?" she asked.

I put my finger to her lips.

"Trust me," I said.

Sadie handed me a basket and I walked around the kitchen, filling it with fruit, cheese, some cold meat I found in the fridge. I rummaged around and found a bottle of white wine, which I took after throwing a questioning glance at Grant, who just nodded.

"Come," I said, walking out of the kitchen.

We walked back through the sitting area and I grabbed the blanket off the couch before heading for the stairs. I took her up to the attic, which I was using as additional storage for some of my pieces. I pushed open the door and felt around on the wall for the light switch. Flipping it on, I took her hand and brought her in.

She stood there for a moment, looking around. Within two seconds, Loki, the grey and white resident cat, streaked past her legs and ran into the attic. Lainey let out a little shriek and squeezed my hand. I laughed.

"Lainey, meet Loki."

Lainey laughed, trying to catch her breath.

"That thing scared the shit out of me," she said.

"Best little mouser around," I said, walking over to pet him.

As Lainey walked around the room, examining all the furniture, I spread out the blanket on the floor and unpacked the food.

"This is all yours." A statement, not a question.

"You can tell," I said, pleased.

"Of course I can tell."

She whipped around to look at me.

"You're such a fool," she whispered.

"Don't start, Lainey. Sit down, let's have a nice lunch."

She sat down across from me on the blanket, tucking her legs up underneath her. She reached for her empty glass and held it out as I uncorked the wine and poured it. Then I handed her a piece of cheese, which she popped in her mouth. A smile spread across her face.

"I haven't had Quebec cheese in ages. Nothing compares."

"We've got a nice variety here, so you should be good."

She poked through the contents on the blanket, picking up the cheese knife and sampling a different wheel. She was definitely in her happy place. I wondered if LA Lainey was different from Mountain Valley Lainey, then shook off the thought. It didn't really matter.

"Do you like LA?" I asked her.

"When I have work, I love it. When I don't, I spend my time worrying about the next time I'll work." She let out a soft laugh. "Look, I don't *love* LA, but I do love what it has to offer me."

"That makes sense," I conceded.

I wanted to tell her how much Mountain Valley had to offer me, but the last thing I wanted to do was set her off again, so I poured another glass of wine instead.

"I'll admit, it is kind of nice to be here right now, with you," she said quietly.

I glanced over at her. She was looking down, studying some invisible bit of lint on her knee. She must have felt me looking at her, though, because she raised her eyes and held my gaze. I inched a little closer.

"I've thought about calling you so many times," I said.

"Why didn't you?" she asked.

"I don't know. I figured you'd moved on."

"Well, I have, of course, but that doesn't mean I wouldn't love to hear from you. We had something special, Logan. I won't ever forget that. But we were eighteen. We're thirty-five now. A lifetime has passed in those years."

She had moved on. Was she seeing someone? Why wouldn't she have told me?

"I'm not seeing anyone," she said. "God, you're so transparent."

I didn't know whether to be relieved or pissed, so I went with relieved. It was hard work, keeping things on an even keel with Lainey. It was only one o'clock and I was already exhausted.

"I just meant I haven't been sitting in California pining for you. As I'm sure you haven't been doing here. I didn't mean I was involved."

"I got it. Thanks."

There was a quick knock on the door and then Grant poked his head in.

"Hey, I don't mean to disturb you, just wanted to let you know I just got word the plows are coming through. You may be able to get out of here soon, not that we wouldn't love to have you stay another night—"

Lainey jumped up.

"That's sweet, really, but I'd love to settle into my place by tonight. How long do you think it'll be before the plows come around?"

"Not long," he said. "Maybe an hour?"

I got up and started packing up the basket. Lainey knelt down to help and we both reached for the wine bottle at the same time. Our hands brushed, and while I wouldn't say fireworks went off, there was definitely something there. Whether it was nostalgia or something else, I didn't know. What I did know was that she felt it, too. Because as transparent as Lainey thought I was, I could just as easily see through her.

CHAPTER SIX

Lainey

Once the snow stopped falling, the mountains were absolutely breathtaking. As Logan navigated carefully along the empty roads, I took in the white-capped peaks, the dusted evergreens, the impossibly blue sky—all of it was picture-perfect.

"What are you thinking?" Logan asked, breaking the silence.

"I'd forgotten how beautiful this all was."

He didn't say anything in response. I'd already gotten the feeling he was scared to say anything to me. For the life of me, I couldn't figure out why I'd jumped down his throat so many times in the past twenty-four hours. He'd done nothing wrong, yet it was obvious I'd put him on edge. I thought about how I could rectify that, then decided to file it away for later, when I had more time and a clearer head.

We pulled into the parking lot of the bus station and he killed the engine.

"Listen," he said. "I don't have much going on today, I could help you get settled if you need—"

"Logan, you've already done so much. I'll be fine, really."

He looked down at his hands.

"That doesn't mean we won't see each other again," I said. "Let me settle in, get to work, and then maybe we'll have dinner."

He smiled.

"That sounds great."

We exchanged cell phone numbers before we both got out of the car. He helped me gather my stuff and walked me over to the car rental kiosk. I took my bag from him, then leaned over and kissed him on the cheek.

"Thank you," I said. "For everything. I'll call."

"Okay."

He watched me walk in, then turned to leave.

*

The cottage was perfect. Nestled into a private lot off one of the back roads, it was right on a lake and surrounded by dense forest. After years of noise and pollution in LA, it was like heaven. I laughed out loud as I got out of the car and walked around the property.

I cleared a path to the front door with my boots and unlocked it. I entered the house and smiled again as I took it all in. It was tiny, just one floor with a large living room with bay windows overlooking the lake, a small kitchen, and a mid-sized dining area. It was all open concept, except for the two bedrooms tucked away in either corner of the living room. I dropped my bag, then returned to the car for my supplies.

I'd spent a good two hours in town collecting groceries and whatever else I thought I'd need, including some wood to tide me over until I could arrange for delivery.

A few of my favourite haunts were still around, but mostly everything had been replaced. The old bookstore was still there but closed due to the storm. I'd have to make my way back there. I'd seen surprisingly few people that I knew, but our exchanges had been joyful. I thought about how much older everyone seemed and wondered if they felt the same about me.

I stood outside the door before going in with the final load, taking one last breath of that crisp, clean air, inhaling it deep into my lungs. In some ways, it was good to home.

Once everything was unpacked and organized, I pulled out my computer and placed it on the large writing desk in the living room. That desk had been the reason I'd chosen the cottage. As soon as I saw the picture, I felt an instant pull towards it. My agent had thought I was nuts, agreeing to something so small, but I knew all I needed was that desk.

I stood there, looking at the set-up for a while. Satisfied, I shut the light and walked over to the bedroom. It was close to nine and I was exhausted. I climbed into bed, unable to believe only hours earlier I'd been having a picnic lunch with my high school boyfriend in the attic of a bed and breakfast.

I closed my eyes, and before I could give it another thought, I was out.

*

The next few days passed smoothly. My first morning I got up and started writing, the words flowing easier than they had in months.

I barely noticed the passage of time, day turning into night and vice versa. Sometimes I worked early into the morning and slept through until mid-afternoon, other days I'd wake early and take a brisk walk before settling in to work.

I was shocked at how easily I transitioned from city life to isolation. It was an eerie feeling those first few nights, falling asleep to the sounds of nature instead of honking horns and blaring music. Beth checked in regularly to ensure I was eating properly. I assured her I was taking excellent care of myself and I was.

On Thursday morning, I woke up and decided to go for my usual walk. I peered out the window and saw the snow falling. I slipped on my coat and hat and left the house, pulling the front door shut behind me.

Almost immediately, I had a sense something was off. I looked around but saw nothing. I took a step forward, but beneath the sound of my boots crunching through the snow, I heard a soft sound, almost a whimpering. I stopped and looked around again. Nothing.

I walked a slow path around the house, trying to get closer to the sound, but it was evading me. It was definitely a whimper, punctuated by the occasional soft cry. My heart broke listening to it, and I couldn't imagine what kind of animal it might be. It didn't sound big, but it did sound like it was in pain.

I moved towards the woods, thinking it might have tried to escape when it heard me coming, but as I walked into the trees, I heard the sound behind me, loud and clear. I stopped in my tracks and turned around. There before me was a dog, probably about forty pounds, but he should've been closer to sixty by the size of him. He was mostly black, with white and grey fur woven through his coat. He looked so sad, so miserable. I couldn't tell if he was young or old. I approached him slowly.

I don't know if I expected him to run or stand still. What I didn't expect was for him to approach me, too, just as cautiously as I approached him. We met in the middle, and I saw my earlier mistake. This was definitely a female. And she was hungry.

"Hey, girl," I said, kneeling down. "You okay?"

She just looked at me, ears twitching, tail not raised, but not tucked between her legs, either.

"You need a friend, huh?"

I looked her over. Her coat was filthy and matted, but I could still see a few ribs poking through.

"Maybe a meal?"

I stood up again and started walking back towards the house, intending to bring some food out for her. To my surprise, she followed me, sticking close to my side. I laughed, and we entered the house together.

I kicked off my boots and walked to the fridge, opening it up and rifling around. I pulled out some eggs and cheese and turned on the stove. The dog ambled over and sat at my feet while I scrambled the eggs, giving me the very definition of puppy-dog eyes.

She was so cute, despite being such a mess. I tilted the pan, letting the eggs slide into a bowl, and lowered it to the floor. By the time I stood up, they were gone. I found another bowl and filled it with water, and she took a long, sloppy drink.

"I guess I'm going to need some dog food."

I sat down at the table and watched the dog explore the house, trying to come up with a name for her. It was clear she belonged to no one, and if she ever had an owner, those days were long over. I had no idea how she'd survived so long on her own.

I stood up and walked to the bathroom. She followed me willingly, so I turned on the faucet in the tub. She glanced over at me, then tentatively put her paw into the tub before jumping in. I laughed, delighted. She stuck her head under the faucet and started drinking, letting the water flow all over her head.

I grabbed the shampoo bottle and lathered her up, giving her a good scrub before rinsing her with the removable shower head. I got her dried off but realized I had nothing to brush her with.

"Food and a brush. And a collar and a leash, I guess. Shit. We better drive into town."

CHAPTER SEVEN
Logan

I was walking down Main Street, having just come out of the hardware store. I was thinking of cutting through the square when I saw Lainey emerge from the pet shop, laden down with multiple bags and a dog. I waited a fraction of a second to ensure it was her then hurried over.

"Lainey?"

She turned to me, then looked down at the dog before letting out a nervous laugh.

"Logan. Hey."

"What's going on?"

"Um, I found her. Or, actually, she found me."

"Lainey, that's Mrs. Miller's dog, Bella."

Lainey looked at me, surprised. She blinked

a few times, and I saw a small tear form in the corner of her eye. She gave another quick laugh and wiped it away with her shoulder.

"Oh! Bella." She knelt down, dropped the bags, and scratched the dog's head. "That suits you, doesn't it?"

She stood up again and looked around, then down at all her bags.

"Hm. I wonder if they take returns."

"Lainey, no. Mrs. Miller died last year. You must be renting her old cabin. No one's seen Bella since the day she died. This is a miracle. I can't believe she's still alive."

I knelt down to pet the dog, who leaned in against me, hungry for affection. Mrs. Miller had gone nowhere without Bella, and on the day she died, we'd sent out search parties looking for her, but came up with nothing. It truly was a miracle.

"So...she's mine?" Lainey asked hesitantly.

"Yeah, I guess so."

Lainey let out a delighted laugh and knelt down beside me, taking the dog's head in her hands and touching her nose to the dog's.

"Hear that, Bella? You and me."

The dog licked her face and Lainey laughed. It was the first time since her arrival that I saw her look so fucking happy.

"Come, let me help you with this stuff," I

said.

I grabbed her bags and she led me to her car. We loaded everything in, including Bella, and Lainey shut the door. She turned to me and we stood there awkwardly for a moment, unsure of what to say next.

"How's the writing going?" I asked.

"Fantastic. I'm stuck in a few spots, but otherwise, it's going pretty smoothly. Thanks for asking. How's everything with you?"

"Good. I'm busy with a new commission."

"That's great."

Bella started whining and pawing at the window, causing a smile to break out on Lainey's face.

"Hey," I said. "If you want, I can come by and help you get set up and stuff."

She looked at me and cocked her head.

"You know, that would be great. You know the place?"

I nodded, and she walked around to the driver's side door of her car.

"Great," she said. "I'll see you there."

*

I hadn't been inside the Miller cottage in years. I'd done some work for Mrs. Miller a while back, but as she aged, she took less and less care of the place and stopped calling me. I tried to swing by a few times on my own, but she'd gotten pretty paranoid towards the end and wouldn't let me in.

Clearly whoever took over the place had done some major renovations. The space was all well-used and well-designed. I kicked off my boots and looked around, touching the molding around the doors and windows, and then smiling widely as I turned and saw the desk.

Lainey shook the snow off her coat before hanging it up, then caught my expression and gave me her full attention.

"What's up?" she asked.

I nodded my chin towards the desk.

"I made that," I said.

She stared at me, shocked.

"That's the reason I rented this house."

We both burst out laughing.

I walked over and ran my hand along the top of the desk, the memory of carving it flooding my senses. Fuck, I loved working with mahogany. An even grain, no pockets or voids, and it only got better-looking over time. It filled me with pleasure to know she sat writing at that desk, every day.

Lainey unpacked her bags on the table while

I sat on the floor and played with Bella. Well, more like pet her. She wasn't quite at a point where she felt like playing yet. I figured she must've been about five or six years old at that point. Still plenty of spunk left in her—it just needed to be drawn out. She couldn't have found a better human than Lainey for that.

Lainey walked over, triumphantly waving a dog brush in the air.

"Found it!"

She plopped down on the floor next to me and reached out to pet Bella, who immediately lay down at her feet. Lainey smiled at me, then started brushing her. That dog didn't move a muscle as Lainey worked through each tangle and mat. Instead, she'd occasionally give her a lazy swipe of her tongue, showing her appreciation.

I got up and walked over to the fridge, opening it up and finding six bottles of beer. I glanced at her over my shoulder.

"Beer?"

She nodded, so I grabbed two, opened them, then returned to the living room. I passed one to her as I took a seat on the couch, taking a swig as I watched her patiently brush out the dog.

"You ever have a dog?" I asked her.

"Nope. Always wanted one, though. But my

mom didn't."

"I remember. I meant if you ever got one after moving out west."

She shook her head sadly.

"I wish. My apartment is too small, and I've got a no-pet clause in my lease. Besides, a dog needs space, other dogs, exercise—where I'm living isn't really conducive to all that."

"That's a shame. Look how good you are with her," I said.

She smiled down at Bella, who panted up at her. Lainey set the brush aside and buried her fingers in the dog's thick coat. She leaned down, burying her nose in its neck.

"Yeah. We'll figure it out. Maybe I'll move out to Venice Beach or something."

In a few hours, she was willing to make a concession for a dog she'd just met when she hadn't been able to make one for me after three years of dating. I realized it wasn't the same, but the fact that she was willing to compromise for a dog, no matter how damn sweet it was…it hurt.

I swallowed my pride and my biting comment and took another swig of beer. It was some artisanal stuff she must've found at the general store at the bottom of the hill. They were known several towns out for having the best selection of craft beer. She'd certainly figured shit out quickly, despite all the changes since she'd left.

"Do you know how to take care of her?" I asked. "Not to sound like an asshole or anything—"

"No, no," she interrupted. "I get it. Is it that difficult? A few walks? Feed her a couple of times a day? Let her snuggle me in my bed?"

Bella nuzzled Lainey's palm, angling for some petting. Lainey happily obliged. Then she stood suddenly as if remembering something. She walked over to the table and picked up a large coil of line. She walked back and handed it to me.

"Do you think you could set this up outside? I was thinking between the two tall maple trees? Then she can have a line to run free outside."

I looked at the materials in my hand and laughed.

"You think she's going to run away from you?"

"I don't want to take any chances."

I nodded.

"Okay, I'll take care of it."

I stood up and pulled on my jacket and boots, heading out with Bella at my heels. I grabbed a few things from my truck and got to work.

CHAPTER EIGHT

Lainey

After I finished setting up Bella's bowls and filling them with food and water, I walked over to the window to check Logan's progress. The snow was falling, but he was still there, working to string up the line and attach the carabiners. It would've been an easy job in any other season but winter, and I could imagine him cursing under his breath as he tried to clear a path to the second tree.

I stood there watching him, intending to set up the rest of the dog stuff while he worked, but instead I was glued to the spot. There was something so familiar about his movements, the shape of him, yet at the same time, it all felt new.

I told him I hadn't thought of him romantically in ages, but watching him now, I wondered if that was true. Of course, there'd been the occasional fantasy, but we'd been young and had enjoyed great sex—it was only natural I'd use that as material. Even if it was almost two decades ago.

Just thinking about his hands on me made my entire body flush with heat. The first time we'd kissed we were fourteen, and to this day I hadn't found anyone who kissed me like that. It wasn't a perfect kiss—though we certainly got better over time—but he kissed me like he *knew* me.

Pulling up the memory of that kiss came easy, and my breathing changed as I stood there, eyes shut, falling back into a familiar daydream.

The sound of the door slamming shut behind me, followed by a quick bark, snapped me out of my reverie. I shook my head, as if trying to clear the fog, then offered Bella a smile.

"Find your voice, did you?"

Logan laughed and shook the snow off his hair as he pulled off his coat.

"I'll say. She had quite a bit to say to the birds," he said.

He turned to give Bella a quick scratch on

the head, but she jumped up on him, covering him in her wet paws. He laughed and pushed her down.

"Oh, shit," he said. "I'm soaked."

He laughed some more as he pulled off his T-shirt. I wasn't laughing. I swallowed and willed myself to stay rooted to the spot, despite the gravitational pull I felt towards him.

"Do you, uh, cut down the trees you make that furniture out of?" I asked.

He looked at me, uncomprehending. My eyes fell to his chest and abs. He glanced down and laughed.

"Why thank you, Lainey, it's nice that you noticed—"

Before he could get out another word, I'd crossed the room and covered his mouth with mine. I had no idea what came over me, but the sight of him there, shirtless, mixed with the memory of his touch, was more than enough to make me do the crazy.

His ice-cold hands found the back of my neck, but I didn't even flinch. I was giving off so much heat I barely noticed. His tongue reached out to part my lips and I obliged, wrapping my arms around his waist, running my hands up his muscled back.

He pulled back, just a fraction, and looked me in the eye.

"Lainey?"

"I don't know. Don't question it, please."

He leaned down and kissed me again, deeper this time, with an underlying sense of urgency and profound need. My arms came up around his neck, pulling him down towards me as I pressed myself up against him. I heard him groan as he weaved his fingers through my hair, refusing to let me go.

It was like the years between us were gone, and we were back making out behind the bleachers after one of his football games. I lost myself in him and found the reality perfectly matched the fantasy. The way he held me, the way he stroked the back of my head, the way he was growing hard against me.

He kissed a line towards my ear and then whispered, "I don't have any condoms."

I pulled back and gave him a half-smile.

"I seem to remember that we found plenty of other things to do in the years before I let you take my virginity," I said.

"And some things you wouldn't let me do…"

"Oh, I am past that."

Without another word, Logan dropped to his knees and worked the button on my jeans, unzipping the fly and peeling them down, leaving me in my shirt and panties. He ran his hands up my thighs and I shivered, not from the cold but from the clear sense of déjà vu.

He reached around and cupped my ass with both hands, burying his head between my legs, his nose directly up against my clit. I closed my eyes and gripped his head.

"This might not be the best spot," I murmured.

He rose to his feet and grabbed me around the waist, lifting me as I wrapped my legs around him. He carried me to the bedroom and kicked open the door with his foot.

He stopped at the threshold to kiss me and I started grinding against him.

"You're killing me," he whispered.

"Put me down."

He lowered me to the floor and I peeled off my top as he took off his jeans. We stood there, staring at each other for a few moments, taking in the way our bodies had changed, how they hadn't. He smiled at the scar from my belly ring.

"You took it out," he said.

I shrugged.

"You look fabulous," he said.

He walked over and planted a soft kiss on my lips as he reached behind me to unclasp my bra, which I let fall to the floor. He stepped back again to take me in, closing his eyes briefly and taking a deep breath.

"I cannot tell you how many times I've thought about this moment," he said.

"Stop talking."

I reached out and ran a finger across his chest, down to his happy trail. Scrumptious. His body was definitely older, and not as lean as it had been when he was eighteen, but fuck, was he in shape. Even more so now. This was the kind of body achieved after years of sustained exercise. I wanted to devour it.

I slid my hands into the waistband of his boxer briefs and slid them down, falling to my knees as I did so. He looked down at me, shaking his head.

"No way, me first."

I smiled up at him as I took him in hand, stroking him until he was forced to close his eyes and lay his hand on the top of my head.

"From what I recall," he choked out, "this was not one of your favourite activities."

"Like I said, I'm past that."

I gently licked a straight line along the length of his shaft, starting at the bottom and ending up at the head, after which I proceeded to take him in my mouth. He let out a low, deep sigh, his fingers tightening in my hair, his knees almost buckling.

I smiled around him, taking my time, getting familiar with the territory. It was true we'd had *a lot* of sex in high school, but I'd also been a teenage girl and a little wary of oral sex. It was one of my life-long regrets, actually, that Logan and I had never done this.

I teased him until he started making pained sounds and crying for mercy, then I got down to business as I reached up to cup his balls.

"Oh, fuck," he cried.

I lightly ran my teeth down him, following it with a soothing pass of the tongue. He was putty in my hands and I had no idea how he'd managed to stay on his feet. I glanced up and saw both hands braced against the wall. He caught my eye so I held his gaze. That was one step too far for him, and within a second, he was coming in my mouth.

"Oh, god, Lainey."

He pulled me up to my feet and gently steered me towards the bed. I sat down on the edge, then shimmied up until I was lying against the headboard, wriggling out of my panties in the process. Logan followed me onto the bed, and paused, on his knees, as he took me in.

"Lainey."

I smiled at him and reached out my hand. He took it and lay down next to me, covering my face in soft kisses. I laughed, tickled, and he covered my mouth with his. For the life of me,

I couldn't remember what I'd found funny a moment ago. I closed my eyes and let him kiss me, his mouth moving from mine down my neck, to the hollow place at my collar bone. I arched my back and he ran his hand up my breast, stopping to his pass his thumb over my nipple.

It had been a long time since I'd been with a man, over a year at least. My body was incredibly responsive, waking up to a pleasure it had almost forgotten about. His hand slid down, palm flat against my belly and I raised my hips, eager to feel his touch.

He groaned softly in my ear.

"You feel so good."

I sighed in response and moved against his hand. He dipped his head and kissed my breast before tracing small circles around my nipple with his tongue. My body was on fire, electricity coursing through my veins. It had never felt this good in high school.

His mouth closed around my breast and I held the back of his head, pressing him against me as I rode his hand. He broke away, planting one last kiss on my mouth before sliding down the bed and working himself into position between my legs.

He paused again, just looking at me, as if unable to believe this was happening. I knew exactly how he felt. I ran my hand through his hair, tugging at the curls until he broke into a smile. Then he dipped his head and the rest of the world fell away.

CHAPTER NINE
Logan

Breathless, I crawled up the bed to lie down, collapsing in the spot next to her. I lay my head on her chest, and she stroked my hair as I tried to get myself under control. Lainey. I'd just gone down on Lainey. That had been the one no-no during our relationship, the one line she wouldn't cross. I had no idea what had changed her mind over the years, but I was damn grateful for whatever, or whoever, had done it.

"That was something," she said. I could hear the smile in her voice.

"It certainly was."

We were both silent for a few minutes, until I worked up the nerve to ask what was really on my mind.

"What just happened there?"

Her hand paused on my head, then resumed playing with my hair.

"I'm not sure. I was watching you outside, and I remembered how we used to be, and then you took off your shirt—"

I burst into laughter.

"Really? It's as simple as that?"

She shrugged.

"Honestly, I didn't really think it through." She glanced over at me, nervous. "I'm not saying that this meant that—"

"Relax, it's okay. I get it. It was a moment. I'm glad it happened."

I leaned over and kissed her, then dropped back on my pillow. I felt the entire mattress shift and sink as Bella jumped up, clearly making herself at home. She circled the bottom of the bed a few times and then lay down, keeping her eyes on us as she rested her chin on her paws.

"I think you're stuck with her," I murmured.

"Not a problem," she said, sitting up to give the dog a few pets before climbing under the covers.

"What are you doing?" I asked. "It's like, three o'clock."

"Yup," she smiled. "Nap time."

*

I couldn't remember the last time I'd taken a nap. I leashed up Bella and took her for a walk while Lainey slept, the idea of wasting daylight hours completely foreign to me. As we navigated the freshly fallen snow, the dog more gracefully than I, I thought about what a miracle it was that she was still alive. A lot thinner, to be sure, but I had zero doubt that Lainey would take care of that in no time.

About a kilometre away from the house, I just stopped and burst out laughing. I couldn't believe I was standing there, having just fooled around with my high school girlfriend, and was now walking her dog. It was just too much. I turned back, heading towards the house while thinking about how to play this. She'd made it clear what our romp had meant, or more precisely, what it hadn't meant, and I wasn't about to fuck things up with her. If she wanted to be friends, that was fine. I'd play along. But after an hour in bed with her, my desire to be with her had only deepened.

As I approached the cabin, I wondered if she'd be up for round two. There were so many things I wanted to do with her, to her. I glanced at my car, contemplating driving into town for condoms, but then decided that could wait. I didn't want to lose the moment.

I let myself into the house, kicking off my boots and unleashing the dog. I looked up and saw Lainey sitting at the desk, headphones on, deep in concentration as her fingers flew across her keyboard. I stood there watching her for a few minutes before slipping my boots back on, zipping up my jacket, and easing out the door.

*

"You want to tell me what's going on?" Grant asked.

"Nothing is going on," I said, bringing the hammer down on my thumb. "Shit!"

I was at the B&B, trying to sneak in a few hours of work while I mulled things over. Apparently, I'd been distracted. Sadie came running into the dining room as Grant stood over me, watching with a skeptical look on his face. He put his arm out to stop her from getting too close as I paced the floor, swearing loudly and often.

"Should I get you some ice?" Sadie asked.

I nodded my head, unable to form any polite words. Grant just kept watching me. Ever since I became, for all intents and purposes, parentless, the Andersons had stepped into the role. No matter the job, they kept hiring me so I was always around. I knew my work was good, but it wasn't that good. They just wanted to keep an eye on me. As evidenced by Grant's current behaviour—literally keeping an eye on me.

"Spit it out," I said.

"You're distracted," Grant said. "It's not like you."

"I just want to get this finished, that's all. It's been dragging for years and you need the space back."

Grant nodded, never taking his eyes off me. I tried to ignore him as I pressed the ice to my thumb. Sadie took up her post beside her husband and I knew it was a lost cause. Once the two of them set their mind to something... well, just the fact that I was there was evidence of their combined abilities.

I sat down on my workbench and looked at them.

"Fine. I'm distracted. I've been thinking about Lainey. You happy?"

Sadie suppressed a smile.

"Not happy," Grant said. "But we want you to know we're here. To help."

"Help? How are you going to help? I was here, living my life, and then suddenly she shows up. Now all these old feelings have resurfaced and I know exactly how it's going to play out. She's going to finish this project, pack up, and go home. And I'll still be here, shattered again like the last time."

"You've moved on?" Grant asked, skeptical.

"Yes, of course I have. I date. I've had relationships."

Grant and Sadie exchanged looks.

"What?" I hissed.

"Well, there was Brenda..." Sadie said.

"Let's not talk about Brenda," I said.

"Fine. So you've dated. But Logan, sweetheart, you've never really given any woman a part of yourself," Sadie said.

I felt like I'd had the wind knocked out of me. Was that true? I thought back on my past relationships, of the women leaving because I couldn't commit, or couldn't open up, or was just "emotionally unavailable."

And then I thought about Brenda.

I looked up, both of them regarding me with nothing but love. And I was pissed.

"I gotta get back to work."

They exchanged a quick glance and made a hasty retreat. I picked up the hammer, ignoring the pain in my hand, and finished the job.

CHAPTER TEN

Lainey

It was a bitterly cold day, the wind snapping at my back, but the sky was a clear, bright blue. It was like Mother Nature's cruel joke—make everyone think it was a gorgeous day, then Boom! Gotcha!

I turned up Main Street, wishing I hadn't parked so far away. I'd thought the walk would do me good, but without Bella, walking had really lost all its appeal. I saw Franni's sign up ahead and a wave of nostalgia went through me at the memory of old Mrs. Simon's cinnamon buns.

The bakery had been everything to me as a kid. The first place I spent my own hard-earned money. The place Logan and I used to go and order coffees and danish, thinking we were so grown up. I smiled as I pushed in the door and heard the bell. Bells were everywhere in Mountain Valley.

The first thing to hit me was the smell. It was amazing. I closed my eyes and breathed in, not giving a damn what I looked like. The childhood memories were so overwhelming I reached out to grab hold of the wall so I wouldn't be bowled over.

"Can I help you?"

I opened my eyes and saw a woman standing behind the counter, eyeing me with amusement. She looked vaguely familiar, but I couldn't quite place her. A common occurrence I'd noticed since being back.

"I'm sorry. I'm having a moment. I used to come here as a kid," I said.

"I remember."

I looked at her again, with more intent this time. Who was she?

"You don't remember me?" she asked, laughter dancing in her voice.

I shook my head, slowly.

"It's me, Katie Simon. You used to babysit me when I was a kid."

"Oh my god. Katie! I can't believe it. Look how grown up you are. Shit!"

I ran over and she came out from behind the counter to give me a hug. I pulled back and

80

looked at her again. She must have been about twenty-seven or twenty-eight. She'd been such a great kid, full of spunk and spirit, and fiercely intelligent. What on earth was she still doing here?

"You're wondering what I'm still doing here."

I laughed. Perceptive as always.

"Kind of," I admitted.

"First tell me what you're doing here," she said, reaching behind the counter to grab a croissant for me.

I smiled and took it, taking a bite before going on.

"I'm in town to finish work on a script being produced by Mason Scott's production studio."

She nodded, serious.

"You mean my boyfriend?"

I stared at her, shocked, as the pieces fell into place.

"Holy shit. You're that Katie."

She spread her arms and did a quick curtsy.

"How on earth did that happen?"

She shrugged.

"Well, I came home after college to help my grandmother out here, and when she died, she willed the place to me. I couldn't bring myself to sell it, so I decided to move home permanently and make a go of it. After a couple of years, I brought in my two best friends, Jax and Tess, as partners. They'd been helping me from almost day one, so it made sense."

I nodded, taking it all in. Looking around, I could see where she'd kept her grandmother's mark and where she'd made her own. It was the perfect blend of nostalgic and modern, ideal for a small-town bakery. And the croissant was delicious.

"Where are you staying?" Katie asked.

"I rented Mrs. Miller's cabin. And if you'll believe it, I found her dog."

"Bella? Get out!"

"It's true. Actually, she found me. Walked out one morning and there she was, waiting to rescue me." I smiled at the memory.

Katie went back behind the counter and pulled out a bag, filling it with peanut butter cookies. She handed it to me.

"For Bella, on the house. These are her favourite."

I laughed and took the bag.

"Thanks. But I'm going to need to place a bigger order. Got a pen?"

I spent the next twenty minutes with Katie, and when she told me about her catering business, it pretty much changed my life. I set myself up for meals for the next two weeks. Before I left, we made plans to go for dinner the next week. At our age, the seven years between us was nothing. And it was good to find a friend.

*

INT. ITALIAN RESTAURANT - NIGHT

Lexie sits at the table, waiting for her mother to arrive. She eyes the menu, shutting it and setting it aside.

A knock at the front door made me jump out of my seat. I'd been staring at those two lines on the page for God knew how long, waiting for inspiration to strike. It was the first meeting between estranged mother and daughter in years and it was the one scene in the whole film I'd avoided writing. There was no putting it off any longer.

Except that there was someone at the door. The knock came again, and Bella lifted her head, eyeing me lazily to see if it was worth barking about. I pushed back the chair and made my way to the door.

I saw Logan's truck through the window and paused. I hadn't seen or spoke to him since the night we'd almost slept together. I'd been in a work daze when he slipped out, and neither of us had made the effort to contact the other since. I had no idea what to expect when I answered the door, so I braced myself with a deep breath.

"Logan. Hey."

"Hey. Mind if I come in for a second?"

I moved aside, opening the door wider.

"Of course not."

I gave him some space and he came in, carrying a large box with a postal bag slung over his shoulder. He kicked off his boots and made his way to the living room, dropping the box on the table before pulling off his hat. He then removed the mailbag, placing it on the floor, and unzipped his coat.

I watched in silence as he shed his outer layer, flashes of our last evening together playing in my head. *Relax. You are not eighteen anymore.*

"What's all this?" I asked, surveying the load he'd deposited in my living room.

"Your mom's stuff. I promised I'd bring it by."

My breath caught and I took a step backwards. Logan reached for me as I felt the colour drain from my face. I pushed him away.

"I'm fine."

We both stood there, not a word passing

between us. But we'd never needed words to communicate. We'd always been able to read each other. That's why we'd worked so well together. Now it felt like a curse.

"What are you scared of, Lain?"

I shook my head, blocking him out as I bent down to pet Bella, who was nuzzling my leg.

"Lain, it's me. Talk to me."

I shot up and looked him in the eye.

"Listen, I don't know what you think is going on here, but I don't have to talk to you. I don't want to talk to you about this. You have to stop 'it's me'-ing me. We're not an 'us' anymore. We are two grown people who dated once upon a time."

I bit my lip. I hadn't intended to be so harsh, but it had all just spilled out. I saw the hurt in his eye, felt it in my gut. It was awful.

"Hey. You were there with me the other night—" he started.

"Yes. I was. I'm not denying it was amazing. But nothing has changed between us, Logan. I'm still the woman who lives in LA and you're still the guy who's happy in Mountain Valley. We still fight about every little thing. You're glossing over a lot of shit in order to remember the good times. Why are you doing that?"

In two strides, Logan crossed the room and grabbed me around the waist, his mouth finding mine as he kissed me thoroughly.

"That's why," he said. "Tell me you've found someone else to kiss you like that, and I'll leave right now."

My head was spinning. I had not found anyone else to kiss me like that. It made it hard to think, forget think rationally. I brought my hand to my lips and he smirked, knowing we were feeling the same thing.

"Logan. That's not the point."

"JESUS CHRIST, Lainey. What is the point?" he roared. "What else can possibly matter?"

"We have chemistry. I don't deny that—"

"This is not chemistry."

"I don't deny that we have chemistry. But we have seventeen years gone by, and I'm not ready to jump back into something that could potentially upend my entire life and leave me heartbroken. Again. No. I won't go back there."

He stared at me for a minute, then threw on his jacket, grabbed his hat, and headed for the door. He mumbled under his breath as he shoved his feet into his boots and then he turned to me.

"For as long as I live, Lainey Wise, I will never understand you."

With that, he stormed out of the house.

I sighed deeply, then looked around at the mess he'd left behind. The box, the bag, my imagination running wild with what lay inside. My cell phone started buzzing, skittering across the desk. I walked over to grab it. It was Beth.

"Hey, Elena. Just calling to check in. Everything good?"

I laughed.

"Oh yeah. Everything's just great."

CHAPTER ELEVEN

Logan

"Logan! It's so good to see you. It's been ages."

I looked up from my drink and saw Tess Goldberg approaching. I grinned at her, indicating the empty stool beside me. She slid in.

Tess and I had dated very briefly a few years earlier. She had not been the serious type at the time and we worked well together, but eventually, both realized that even though our goals were the same (a casual relationship), our other interests were not. She was all about partying whereas I was happier staying in with take-out and a good movie on Netflix. Hence our short-lived time together.

Now Tess was in a relationship with Adam Black, the owner of Cagney's, the restaurant in which I was currently drinking. I wasn't alone. Plenty of locals came in just to sit at the bar and watch Bree mix drinks. She was a wizard with the bottles and could make up a drink to suit anyone's mood. Tonight, she'd prepared a drink for me and called "Overdue Reckoning."

"A new thing you've started?" I asked. "Naming your drinks?"

"Nah," Bree laughed. "Just a hat tip to a great book I just read."

Now I glanced over at Tess, who was fiddling around in her purse for her phone. She checked the time and put it down on the bar.

"You waiting for Adam to get off?" I asked.

She nodded and signalled Bree for a drink. She didn't specify what kind. No one ever did anymore.

"How are you doing?" she asked. "I haven't seen you in here for a while."

"I've been busy. Lots of work up at the B&B, and I've got a few pieces of my own I've been working on."

Tess took a sip of her drink and then put it back down on the bar with a little more force than she'd probably intended.

"I totally forgot! I saw your stuff on Instagram. It's really amazing, Logan, to see it all there like that."

"You saw it where?" I asked, confused.

"On Instagram. On your feed. I can't believe how many pieces you've sold already. I'd have you buy my drinks if they weren't already free," she laughed.

I had no idea what she was talking about. She must've read the confused look on my face because she picked up her phone and started tapping away. Then she handed it to me. *Right*. The web thing Lainey had set up. I nodded briefly.

"This doesn't excite you?" she asked, incredulous. "I mean, it's amazing."

"What? My furniture on a website? I don't get it."

"I had a feeling you didn't. Logan. This is your stuff, on Instagram, with some, well, pretty insane pricing, and everyone wants to buy it. There are bidding wars on some pieces."

I reached for her phone again and she handed it over. I scrolled through the posts, unable to believe what I was seeing.

"You didn't do this?" she asked.

I shook my head, still scrolling, speechless.

"Who did?" she probed.

I looked up.

"Lainey."

She looked at me blankly for a moment.

"Lainey? Katie's friend?"

"Katie's friend? What are you talking about?" I asked.

"Katie mentioned her coming by the bakery the other day. Apparently, she used to babysit Katie."

I laughed. I'd forgotten all about that. Katie had idolized Lainey back then. Who hadn't?

"How do you know her?" Tess asked.

"We used to date in high school."

"Get out."

"I'm serious."

"Whoa. Okay. That's something completely separate we've got to unpack. But for now, you've got to deal with these sales. Okay. Let's go through this. Lucky for you, I'm here. We're going to make you some money." She looked up and met Bree's eyes. "Another round, please. And keep them coming!"

*

It had been three days since I'd sat at that bar with Tess, and I'd become a madman, checking that damn Instagram account four or five times a day. Or an hour. Whatever. I couldn't believe how easy it was to sell furniture.

I walked around my shop with my pad, scribbling names on sheets of paper and sticking them to various pieces. A dresser here, a vanity there, and many, many tables. People really liked tables.

I marvelled at the lengths some people were willing to go through for something they wanted. I was shipping a table off to Portland. Portland! Were there no furniture stores in the state of Maine?

Between finishing up at the B&B, taking care of orders, and now taking commissions, things were crazy busy. So I was completely unprepared when Nick Felton came in and asked if I was interested in a job. I put down my pad and gave him my full attention.

Nick was a few years younger than me, but both of us stayed in Mountain Valley. He was in construction for a while, but when movies started coming in to film occasionally, he learned how to be a grip and started working in the camera department. He now shifted between gigs, so when he said he had work, I naturally assumed he meant construction.

"I'd love to help you out, Buddy. Really. But I'm swamped these days. Maybe I can hook you up with someone else? Any idea who did the work out at the Miller cabin? Place looks great."

"Nah. Not a clue. But hear me out before you say no. This could be a lot of fun."

I pulled out a deep brown, carved mahogany chair and offered him a seat. I jumped up on the closest dresser and let him have his say.

CHAPTER TWELVE

Lainey

I was sitting on my living room floor, surrounded by letters and journals I'd yet to look at. For the past two days, I'd come into this room and done exactly the same thing: sit down, pick up a letter, unfold it, then put it back again. For some reason, I couldn't bring myself to start.

I had tried writing. It was useless. The entire cottage was saturated with my mother's presence, and until I dealt with it, nothing else was happening. I was so pissed at Logan for putting me in this position, and so close to the deadline.

Bella wandered over and collapsed in a heap beside me. She lay her head across my legs and I reached for a journal. It was the first one, as far as I could tell, marked with the year before I was born. I took a deep breath, opened it, and began reading.

This is for my daughter. Or son, though I feel in my soul that you'll be a girl. I want you to know that even as you grow, I already love you more than anything or anyone else in the entire world. Nothing will ever come between us. And it's important to know you were conceived in love.

I put down the book, a tear already making its way down my cheek. I took another deep breath and tried to get a grasp on my emotions. It was like my mother was talking to me, and I could tell the story she was about to tell was an important one. I surveyed the floor in front of me—six journals, stacks of letters. I glanced over at my laptop sitting on the desk with its blank screen. I turned my attention back to the journals. I'd better get cracking.

*

"Oh my god, Katie, this place is spectacular. I can't believe it exists in Mountain Valley."

I looked around the restaurant, stunned at the beautiful decor and lively action taking place at the bar. This place was definitely not from my time. Katie just laughed and took my hand, leading me towards a table near the back.

"This is Cagney's. It's owned by Adam, Tess's boyfriend. And the chef, Liam, is absolutely stellar. That's his girlfriend, Maggie, over by the bar."

Katie pointed towards a cute redhead sitting at the bar nursing a drink while laughing with the bartender.

"I guess that's how you managed to snag a reservation on a Friday night?" I asked.

"Yup. Also, running the town's best bakery and dating Mason Scott doesn't hurt, either."

"Where is your famous boyfriend this evening?" I asked.

"He's out of town. Have you met yet?"

"Not in person, no. But we've had quite a few conversations over the phone. I was so surprised when I heard he'd planted roots here, but in retrospect, it was a great idea. It's a perfect location."

"It really is," Katie agreed. "Revenue has gone up across almost all local industry as a result. Mason had a vision, and he's going to pull it off."

"It hasn't even been that long, has it?"

"Nope. Paint's not even dry on the studio walls and yours will be the second film to shoot under the banner."

The waiter came around with appetizers,

even though we hadn't ordered. I leaned over towards Katie.

"I don't remember seeing a menu," I whispered.

She just laughed.

"You won't. Liam knows we're here. He's going to make us whatever he damn well pleases. Just enjoy."

*

We were halfway through dessert before I had the guts to broach the subject of my mother's bombshell. There was no reason for me to tell Katie about it, but I needed to talk to someone and that someone couldn't be Logan. Things were confusing enough with him already. This was the second time Katie and I had gone out and we had really hit it off. I decided to ignore my usual modus operandi and open up to another human being.

"You mean, he just dropped off a bunch of your mom's stuff?" she asked.

"Pretty much."

"Have you looked at it?"

"I started."

I used my fork to play with the last piece of cheesecake on my plate. Katie didn't push, just sat silently, waiting until I was ready to go on.

"It's like this six-volume story of my childhood, or the early years, anyway. I only read half of the first one, but it was enough to answer a lot of questions I've been carrying around my entire life."

"About your dad?" she asked quietly.

I nodded.

"Wow. That's heavy, Lainey."

I looked up at her.

"He's a poet. And they were in love."

Katie's eyes widened and she reached across the table to take my hand. At that moment, a tiny woman with a head full of blond curls dropped onto the bench next to Katie and pushed her over with her hip.

"Hey. Am I interrupting anything?"

Katie shot her a look, then smiled at me.

"Lainey, this is my friend and business partner, Tess Goldberg. Tess, this is my old... friend, Lainey Wise."

Tess's eyes widened.

"Elena Wise, Hollywood screenwriter?"

I laughed.

"One and the same. You've seen some of my films?" I asked.

"I've seen all your films. Man, Katie knows the coolest people. Well, not just Katie, I guess. I had drinks with your old high school boyfriend the other night."

Katie and I exchanged quick glances and I tried to play it cool, but I doubt I succeeded.

"Pardon me?"

"Logan Matthews. We were having drinks the other night and I mentioned his Instagram account. He told me you set it up for him. Good job. He's been doing crazy business. He didn't even know!" Tess laughed, delighted at his innocence.

I sat there, stunned, trying to process all this new information at once. Tess glanced up and saw her boyfriend across the room. She waved and moved to get up, but I put my hand out.

"Wait. Can you just wait? I need to hear more."

Tess laughed and sat back down.

"Sure thing. What can I tell you?"

"How do you know Logan?"

"Well, we both live here. But also we dated for a bit two, maybe three years ago."

That felt like a slap across the face.

"Was it serious?" I managed to ask.

She shook her head and laughed.

"Logan Matthews, serious? No. It was not. Not that I was looking for anything serious, either. But we just didn't work out for other reasons. Different interests."

"Why is the idea of him having a serious

relationship so funny?" I asked, my brain latching onto that one tiny detail.

"Well, you'd have to ask him, but from my experience, he's not really there with you, you know? I mean, he's great in the sack and everything, as I'm sure you know, but it's like, his focus was never entirely on you. I'm sure you get it. You dated him, too." She paused. "Although, there was that one woman—"

"She was nothing," Katie interrupted.

I didn't get it. I didn't get it at all. Logan was the most vulnerable person I knew. He carried his heart outside his body, in his two hands. I knew this because he handed it to me once, trusting me to take care of it. How could this be the same man? There had to be a mistake.

I chose to ignore the remark about him being great in bed. My brain didn't know what to make of that.

"Right. Thanks. And he mentioned me?"

"Well, not directly. I kind of pieced it together. But I'd seen his stuff blow up on Insta, and when I congratulated him, he was completely clueless. I've been helping him out ever since, showing him how to upload stuff and price it properly. Well, exorbitantly, really, but whatever. You did it first, and it worked." Again, she laughed.

Adam walked over and looked down at her

expectantly. She grinned up at him, a guilty look on her face.

"Sorry, girl talk," she said.

He leaned down and they shared a brief kiss. She was smiling when he pulled away. She let out a soft sigh and then turned back to me.

"Anyway, glad to tell you more, but I'm not sure there's much more to say. It was a pleasure to meet you. Hope to see you again soon."

And with that, she was gone.

CHAPTER THIRTEEN

Lainey

Roughly two weeks after I arrived in Mountain Valley, I had my first meeting with Mason Scott and Nina Laurie, the director. I was in a first-degree panic, due to the script not being finished, but realistically I still had two weeks on my deadline. It would all be a matter of seeing how good I was at bluffing.

It was a relatively mild day for a northern winter, and I took advantage by wearing a lighter sweater. I tended to sweat under pressure, and I needed all the help I could get for this meeting. I threw on a pair of jeans and kissed Bella goodbye before heading out the door. It wasn't too far a drive to the studio, but given the winter road conditions, I wasn't taking any chances.

As I drove up to the old Merson Warehouse, the location of Mason's new production studio, I had to pull over and take a moment. So many of my teenage memories were housed in those buildings. The overhead sign may have been changed to read Scott-Free Productions, a nod to his vow not to star in any of his own productions, but he'd retained the original structure and feel of the buildings. I smiled, thinking what a wise businessman he must be to know he was messing with a cherished landmark.

I parked the car and got out, walking over to the guard's station to check myself in. The guard pointed me to the right building, and I made my way over. I laughed out loud when I entered through the front door and saw a sign pointing to Lover's Lane. Sure enough, it led to a spot in the building where we'd all made out as teenagers. Katie must have had a hand in all of this.

I walked down the corridor and turned into the large studio space, the one they were prepping for the interiors of my film. Prep wasn't due to start for another couple of weeks, but there was already action, as evidenced by the massive amounts of lumber strewn about the room. I stopped in the centre of the mess and looked around, trying to picture what this would all look like in a few months' time.

I heard voices approach from behind and I turned, prepared to greet Mason. We'd never met face-to-face, but of course, I knew what he looked like. Who didn't?

I was greeted by the actor's million-watt smile, but right beside him, chatting away oblivious to my presence, was Logan. The shock on my face must have been evident because Mason rushed across the room, concern in his eyes.

"Elena, right? Is everything okay?"

I nodded, mutely, and just stared at Logan, who was looking right back at me. I shook it off, focusing my attention on Mason.

"Yes, absolutely. Sorry. I didn't mean to interrupt you. Pleasure to finally meet."

I put out my hand and Mason took it, shaking it enthusiastically. Then he nodded his chin towards Logan.

"You're not interrupting at all. My apologies about Logan. We were just going over some final plans. I called him in at the last minute to get the studio ready so we'd be on time. I understand you know each other." He smiled as he said that last bit, and while everything in me wanted to scream, I had to play it cool.

"Yes, of course," I said, smiling at Logan.

He gave me a quick smile in return, but I

could see the hurt still in his eyes. I did not have time for this. Nor did I have the emotional energy to expend. I had to save all of that for the difficult script conversation ahead.

Mason's phone rang and he looked down at the screen before casting an apologetic look in my direction.

"I've got to take this. I'm sorry. Give me five minutes and we'll get started."

With that, he walked out of the studio, talking into his phone. I turned back to Logan, who was still looking at me.

"What do you want me to say?" I asked.

"Not a damn thing, I guess."

"What are you even doing here?"

"You heard the man," he said. "They called me in on a contract. I didn't really have the time, but I knew this was for your film, so I agreed."

I sighed. Why did he always do this?

"Thank you, Logan. Really. But I'm sure they could've found someone else. You shouldn't let anything get in the way of your core business."

He snorted.

"Yeah. That's fitting advice coming from you."

I closed my eyes and counted to ten. When I opened them, he was gone.

*

The meeting with Mason and Nina went as well as it could have under the circumstances. They were very patient and didn't push. I, on the other hand, was very evasive and noncommittal when it came to specific questions.

In truth, the script was pretty much complete. Save for the one pivotal scene. The problem was, I still felt it lacked emotional depth, and while I trusted the actors to get it right, I also knew they needed something from me to get them there.

I got up from my desk, pushing my laptop aside. It was useless. I made my way back to the living room, to the spot that had been calling to me all day. I sat on the couch and picked up the third journal. Reading them had given me an entirely new perspective on my mother. Things she had never spoken to me about were spilled across these pages. The secrets of my childhood were being revealed, and I couldn't even confront her about it.

She'd met my father when he came to Mountain Valley on a year-long writing retreat. He was a young poet who showed great promise and had already won several prizes. According to her, they fell in love at first sight.

They'd met on the ski hill. She'd helped him up after a fall and they'd skied down the rest of the run together. From that moment, they were inseparable. It was clear from some of the entries that my mother had inscribed the books to me as an afterthought, that she'd had no intention of anyone else reading them at the time of writing. I glossed over the more intimate entries, always keeping a keen eye out for important details.

I hit the fourth journal by the time they had their first and only argument. Eight and a half months after they met, it was time for my father to return home. He begged my mother to go with him, but she refused, saying that Mountain Valley was her home. There were pages upon pages of tear-stained entries, and hidden in one of them was the suspicion that she was pregnant.

A month after he left, my mother's suspicions were confirmed. He was still writing to her every day, but she never revealed the pregnancy. She didn't want to hold him back when he was on the verge of becoming something great. She believed his destiny was the most important thing. She loved him too much to ever be the one to tie him down.

What a load of bullshit.

She was young, pregnant, and alone. My mother had moved to Mountain Valley after college in a desperate attempt to get out of the controlling environment her parents had created at home. She had friends and a job, she'd created a life for herself, but ultimately, when it came to raising a child, she'd be alone.

I spent hours reading through those journals. A few months after I was born, she wrote to him to tell him she'd met someone, married, and was pregnant. So he knew she had a child, but he never knew I was his.

CHAPTER FOURTEEN
Logan

I was standing in the finished studio, putting away the last of my tools, when Katie walked in and let out a low whistle.

"Wow, Logan, look what you've done," she said.

I smiled and continued packing up.

"I can't tell you how appreciative Mason is. I don't know what we would've done," she continued.

"It's my pleasure, really," I said.

She paused, studying me, and I could tell something was on her mind.

"Spit it out, Katie," I said.

"I was just wondering if you'd spoken to Lainey recently."

I sighed and sat down on a nearby

workbench.

"It's just that, it's quite a bombshell you dropped on her. It's taking her a bit to process it all."

I looked up.

"Has she read them all?" I asked.

Katie nodded.

"Have you?" she asked.

"No. Of course not. I saw what they were and put everything away for her."

We sat in silence. I looked around, surveying my work, looking for the faults.

"It's not that I didn't want to, it's just that things ended pretty badly between us," I ventured. "And then we bumped into each other here and it didn't go much better."

"Look, I don't want to get in the middle here. You're both adults. All I'm saying is she's on a tight deadline and she's got a lot on her mind. This is a lot for her, and no one else knows her like you do."

With that, Katie smiled and walked out of the studio.

I sat there a while longer, going over my last meeting with Lainey, but my thoughts kept getting interrupted by the memory of our time in bed. Would I be able to separate the two? Untangle my old girlfriend from the woman who needed my friendship?

I pulled out my phone.

Lain. Let's talk.

I waited, not taking my eyes off the screen until I saw those three dots appear.

When?

*

A few hours later, I found myself standing out in the falling snow, knocking on Lainey's door. I could hear Bella barking and was reminded that despite everything, Lainey was wasn't truly alone.

She opened the door and damn, she looked exhausted. I wanted to gather her up in my arms and put her to bed for days. I clenched my fists and walked in, dropping an awkward kiss on her head as I passed her.

"Hey," I said.

"Hey. Thanks for coming by," she added.

I shrugged off my coat and kicked off my boots, following her into the living room where all the journals and letters were laid out across the floor, sorted into some kind of order.

"I see you dug in," I said, nodding towards the piles.

She nodded, saying nothing.

"Come on, Lainey, talk to me."

Her expression shifted as her mouth formed into a tight line. It was subtle, but I recognized it as the first sign of her shutting down, so I opted to retreat. I headed for the kitchen and opened the fridge.

"Beer?" I called.

"Sure. But we're not going to end up in bed again."

I nodded solemnly and removed two bottles from the fridge. I walked back into the living room and sat down on the couch, ignoring the elephant in the room. I handed her a bottle and she took it, sitting down beside me.

"Studio's done," I said.

"That's great. Thanks, really. I'm sorry I jumped down your throat the other day. I think I was just nervous. First meeting and everything."

"It's okay. I get it. I'm more interested in getting past the fight before that one."

She heaved a heavy sigh, but the lines around her mouth had eased.

"Can we just put a pin in that one? Please?"

I put out my hand as a peace offering and she took it. Her hand was warm, relaxed, and I knew I was back on safe ground. It was amazing how little had changed about her, how in tune I still was with her moods. I wondered if she was able to read me as easily.

"How's the writing going, or is that off-limits, too?" I asked.

She let out a soft laugh.

"It's actually going a lot better. I think I've gotten a lot of insight into these characters since reading through my mother's journals. I mean, the stories aren't the same, but a lot of the motivations are, and I was able to use what I found to help strengthen the script, so thank you, I guess is what I'm trying to say."

I smiled. That was a totally unexpected answer, but I was glad to take it. I took a swig of my beer and waited to see if she was going to say anything else.

"She knew who my father was," she said quietly.

I looked over at her. Her head was down and she was focused on peeling the label from her beer bottle. I still said nothing.

"They were in love. He was here for a short time, and when he left, she wouldn't go with him. By the time she found out she was pregnant, he was gone, and she didn't want to tie him down. Thought he was destined for greatness."

"Was he?"

"Yeah." She laughed again. "Turns out he was. I looked him up. Colm Shepherd. He's a poet. A really well-known one. Won a bunch of prestigious awards and shit."

She was silent as she finally freed the last bit of label from the damp bottle. She held it up victoriously before crumpling it in her hand and tossing it on the coffee table.

"He's still alive."

"Holy shit." I couldn't stay silent any longer. "Lain. What are you going to do?"

"I think I'm going to write to him. He knows I exist; he just doesn't know that I'm his. My mom lied, told him she got married and had a baby. So in his mind, I'm a couple of years younger." She snorted. "There's a silver lining for you. In someone's mind, I'm only thirty-three."

I sat there, trying to process everything she was telling me. Lainey Wise had a father, she knew who he was, and he was alive. Who her father was had been the mystery of her life, and she was on the verge of solving it.

"Let's see some stuff he wrote," I said.

"Published or unpublished?" she asked.

I looked at her, confused.

"Well, there are all the books of poetry, but then there's all this." She indicated the letters littered across the floor.

"Those are poems?" I asked, incredulous.

"Yup. That he wrote for my mom." Lainey grabbed a pile of letters and stood up. She started pacing, tossing envelopes left and right. "They loved each other. Why the hell did she let him go? Why did I grow up without a father for no reason?"

"She let him go because she loved him," I said softly.

Lainey stopped pacing and studied me, her eyes narrowing. By the way her eyebrows knit together, I could tell she was putting the pieces of the puzzle together.

"You identify with my mom," she said without the trace of a question in her voice.

"I do. I know exactly why she did what she did."

"You loved me, and you just let me walk away?" she asked.

"What do you think happened?" I asked, truly curious.

"I thought our love just wasn't strong enough. That if it had been, one of us would've been willing to bend. But our own futures were more important at the time." She shrugged. "We were high school sweethearts."

"You really believe that?" I asked.

I got up and walked over to her, taking both her hands in mine, feeling the current of electricity pass between us.

"You don't feel that?" I asked. "You don't look into my eyes and feel exactly what I'm feeling?"

She pulled her hands out of mine and walked to the kitchen, opening the fridge and retrieving a couple more beers.

"I think I'm going through a lot of shit right now and you're a comforting presence."

Ouch.

CHAPTER FIFTEEN
Lainey

I handed Logan the beer and took a swig of my own. I hated when he touched me like that. Of course I felt it. Did he think I'd done anything else besides replaying our night together over and over in my mind?

How had I ended up here? I had left Mountain Valley, carved out a life for myself with friends and a kickass career. Now I was back in my hometown, sitting in my living room drinking beer with my high school boyfriend, discovering the truth behind the biggest lie of my life.

And all I could think about was kissing him. I had to steer this ship in a different direction.

"So I hear from Tess that business is going well," I said.

His eyes lit up.

"Yes. Holy shit. That Instagram thing really worked out. I can't thank you enough. And I've met some amazing artists there, too. You were totally right."

"I'm happy to have helped. And it's great that Tess has taken over."

He paused, eyeing me carefully.

"She's just a friend."

"Oh, I thought she'd said you'd dated."

"We did. Years ago. We're friends now." He smiled slightly. "You jealous?"

I snorted.

"Please. Like I said, high school sweethearts. Besides, she's clearly in love with Adam."

"That is very true."

He polished off the last of his beer and set the bottle on the table.

"Can I look at some of these?" he asked, indicating the letters.

I glanced at the clock on the wall.

"A few, sure. I've got to get back to work soon."

Bella wandered over and nuzzled my leg. I reached down to pet her and she sat on my foot. She'd grown very attached to me in the short time we'd been together.

"Absolutely. I had an exhausting day, too. But with the beers, I'm thinking it's better I wait a bit before hitting the road."

"Make yourself comfortable."

Logan picked up the first pile of letters and sat down on the couch. I watched him for a minute, then walked over to my desk and took a seat. Something he'd said about meeting people on Instagram gave me an idea. I picked up my phone and opened the app, going to the search screen and entering my father's name. Sure enough, he had an account.

I glanced over at Logan, engrossed in the letters, and then hesitated for all of three seconds before composing my private message.

Hi. My name is Lainey. I'm Greta Wise's daughter. I was wondering if you'd like to talk?

I hit send and then went back to my feed, scrolling through the new posts in search of cute dog videos. About two minutes later I saw the notification. My heart sped up. I clicked.

Lainey. It would be my pleasure to meet with you. Where are you?

I sat there, staring at the message. From my father. I took a deep breath and glanced over at Logan. He was fast asleep, snoring lightly as he held one of the letters loosely in his hand. It had been five minutes. He hadn't been lying when he said he was exhausted. I swallowed and looked back down at my screen.

Well, meeting would be kind of tough, since I live

in Mountain Valley, Quebec. But we could talk over the phone.

I hit send and waited. And waited. And waited.

He never sent back another message.

I put my phone down on the desk and flipped up the screen of my laptop. I pulled up my script and stared at the page. I thought about how it felt to have made first contact with my father, a man I'd known nothing about just a few days earlier. He'd been a complete mystery to me, almost non-existent, save for the workings of biology. And now we'd had an exchange.

I started writing. For the first time since taking on the project, I was beginning to understand the idea of an estranged relationship. And as I wrote, it occurred to me that by hiding this from me my entire life, my mother and I hadn't been as close as I'd thought. It made me angry, but it also gave me fuel.

I worked on that scene for hours before finally closing my laptop and checking my phone one last time. Colm had never replied. Maybe I'd shocked him. Maybe he'd regretted his quick reply. Did he even know my mother was dead? Should I have led with that? When was the last time they were even in touch? The letters stopped when I was around five. There may have been more somewhere, but they weren't part of the bounty that Logan had brought me.

I stood up and walked through the living room to get to my bedroom. I saw Logan fast asleep on the couch and started, having completely forgotten he was there. I picked up a blanket and covered him before remembering I had to let Bella out.

I turned back and opened the front door, watching her trot out into the freshly fallen snow. She quickly did her business then came back inside, waiting patiently on the welcome mat for a cookie. I wasn't sure who was better trained.

I shut the door behind her and we both went off to my room. I got ready for bed and climbed in, keenly aware of the fact that Logan was on the couch, just feet away from me. For almost twenty years, there had been no men of consequence in my life and I'd been happy. Now there were two and I was more confused than ever.

*

The smell of bacon wafted into my bedroom,

waking me from a deep sleep. I rolled over and picked up my phone. Seven a.m. I sighed and got out of bed, finding my robe and tying it closed before venturing out into the common area.

Logan was at the stove, singing to himself as he cracked the eggs. I smiled and enjoyed watching him, undetected. I should've known it wouldn't last. Within a minute, he turned to me and grinned.

"You're up early," I said.

"Been up since four. Read most of the letters. He's a real poet, Lain. Like, his shit is good."

"I know," I said, pulling a chair up to the table and sitting down. "I wrote to him last night."

"Did you?"

Logan turned off the stove and slid the eggs onto two plates, which already contained the bacon. He pulled the toast out of the toaster and brought everything to the table. I picked up the bottle of orange juice and poured some into the two empty glasses he'd already set out.

"I did. He wrote back right away, but it's been radio silence ever since. I think I freaked him out."

"Did you tell him you were his daughter?"

"Of course not! I'm not an idiot."

"I didn't mean to imply—"

"Good bacon, Logan. You always made the best bacon."

That little peace offering earned me a genuine smile. I dug into the meal and we both ate heartily.

"I'm sorry I crashed last night," he offered.

"That's okay. You were obviously exhausted."

"Yeah. But those letters, Lain. They're beautiful."

"I know."

I finished eating and carried my plate to the sink. As I turned back, I caught Logan slipping Bella a piece of bacon off his plate. I shot him a look and he grinned sheepishly.

"For that," I said. "You can take her out on her morning walk."

He stood up, laughing.

"Fair enough."

I left the two of them to their business as I went to shower and get ready for the day. When I came back into the room, Logan still had his coat on, having already walked Bella and now ready to leave. I walked over to unleash Bella, and we reached for her at the same time. I turned away.

"Lainey."

I said nothing, just let him unleash the dog. When he was done, he took my hands and placed them against his chest. I could feel the warmth coming off him, through his jacket. I swallowed, unsure what he was hoping to accomplish.

"Why are you running from this, Lainey?"

"We're not doing this now," I said.

He dropped my hands and studied me.

"Funny," he said. "You were always the one willing to take such big risks, now you won't even take a small one with me."

I looked him dead in the eye.

"Because now I know what's at stake."

*

After Logan left, I spent most of the day working on the script and then decided to head out in the late afternoon. It was a mild day and I wanted to take advantage. They seemed to be few and far between.

The writing was much easier now and since I'd gotten over the initial hump of figuring out the reunion scene, it was really just a matter of revising and rewriting until I got it perfect. Beth had been calling nonstop, so I finally sent her the pages. That shut her up.

I opted to leave Bella at home, as it was already past sunset. As I pulled out of the driveway, I realized I had no idea where I was going. I headed for Main Street and took a walk through the square. I hadn't been the only one with that idea, and it seemed like the place was overflowing with people. There were families and couples, toddlers and teens—the entire town had come out to play.

When I started getting cold, I returned to my car and headed for Cagney's. I figured I'd have a drink at the bar, maybe bump into Tess or Katie. When I got there, the place was hopping, but Jen, Adam's second-in-command, found me a seat right away. Bree smiled when she saw me and started mixing a drink.

I sat next to two guys dressed in wool sweaters, still sporting their ski pants. They were both very blond and very sunburned. Clearly tourists.

"Hey, luv," one of them said, turning to me. Australian.

I smiled politely then turned to Bree as she handed me my drink.

"What is it?" I asked.

She shrugged, smiled, and walked away. That was the thing with Bree—her drinks were famous around Mountain Valley and no one ever ordered anymore. She just made whatever came to mind, and everyone loved it. She claimed it was her psych degree, that it enabled her to read people and know just what they'd like. The incredible part was that she'd only been living in Mountain Valley for a year. It was a small town, but to have blended in so seamlessly in such a short time was truly remarkable.

I took a sip and smiled. Delicious. And potent. I sipped slowly, remembering my car outside.

"Ya live round here?" Aussie guy asked.

"Not far," I said, noncommittally.

He turned to his friend.

"She's a shy one, ain't she?"

His friend leaned over and looked me right in the eye.

"How bout a little Aussie kiss then, luv?" he asked.

I raised an eyebrow. I should've kept quiet, but I couldn't.

"What's an Aussie kiss then?"

"Why, just like a French one, but down under."

He and his mate burst into hysterics as I scooped up my drink, slid off my stool, and made my way to the other end of the bar. I'd spotted the couple leaving from the corner of my eye and swooped down before anyone else could claim the spot. Hanging out with a couple of foreign bros had not been my intention when leaving the house.

I felt someone drop down in the seat beside me and looked over. It was Liam, the restaurant's chef. He was still in uniform, so I assumed he was on a quick break. He signalled for Bree, then turned and flashed me a smile.

"Hey, Lainey, right?"

"Yes. How'd you know?"

He shrugged.

"Been hearing a lot about you. Not too many people around I don't know. My girlfriend Maggie is friends with Tess and Katie and—"

"Small town. Right. Got it. I've heard lots about you, too. And your food is amazing."

He grinned and ran his hand over his head. His forearms were huge and tattooed. I'd seen Maggie before and tried to conjure up a mental picture of the two of them together. The story of their meeting must have been an interesting one.

We chatted for a few minutes until Bree brought over his drinks. He took them with a smile, then gave me a wink before heading back into the kitchen. Definitely a charmer. Maggie must have had her hands full with that one.

I stayed longer than I thought I would and as the crowd at the bar thinned out, Bree came over to say hello.

I liked her. She was feisty and totally off the beaten path. It was easy to see she did her own thing, regardless of what anyone thought. I'd only met her a few times, but she was the kind of person I could've easily seen becoming friends with. But Mountain Valley didn't seem to attract that kind of person in the years I'd lived there.

By ten o'clock, it was time to head home. I paid my tab, pulled on my coat, and drove the short distance from Cagney's to the Miller cabin. But when I got there, there was another car parked in my driveway. I pulled up, slowly, and took out my phone, dialling 911 just in case.

As I stepped out of the car, I saw the other car's door open as well. A man got out. He was tall, slender, with grey hair that was just long enough to indicate he'd been a hippie in his younger years. I couldn't believe it. It was Colm Shepherd. Standing in my driveway. I looked nothing like him. I walked slowly towards him.

"What are you doing here?" I asked.

"I'm sorry. I'm sorry I didn't respond. Lainey, for years I've been waiting to meet you and as soon as you told me where you were, I just found the next flight out. I realize how intrusive this is. My plan was to call ahead, but, well—"

"It's okay. Slow down." I walked up to the front door and worked my key in the lock. "Come in, we'll have some tea. Or whisky. Or something."

I laughed nervously, no idea how I was going to play this. I kicked off my boots as Bella ran up to greet me. Colm looked over at the dog and smiled, bending down to pet her. I stood there, watching. My father was in my house.

CHAPTER SIXTEEN

Logan

There was nothing like the smell that came from sanding wood to calm my nerves. I ran my hand over the smooth surface of the table, checking for any flaws or inconsistencies. It looked great. I'd made the table to order, built entirely from reclaimed wood, and the finished result was stunning. I was pleased.

I stood up and walked around the table, giving it a final once over before packing it up for shipment. I glanced around at the shop, empty of customers at the moment, but it was a welcome reprieve. Business had been booming and it was all I could do to keep up. The table had been my last outstanding order and I was looking forward to a few days off. I'd already stopped posting pictures on Instagram a few days ago in anticipation.

I heard the buzz of my phone ringing and looked around, trying to locate it. I saw it across the shop on a dresser and walked over to answer.

"Hello?"

"Hello. Is this Logan Matthews?"

"It is. How can I help you?"

I then listened for five minutes as the guy on the other end of the phone offered to hire me to come out and design built-ins for his chalet...in Colorado. I sat there, stunned. He kept talking, filling me in on all the details. I was about to interrupt him when he got to the payment. Gobsmacked quickly replaced stunned.

"Yeah. Of course. When do you need me?" I asked.

There was a brief pause.

"Can you come tomorrow?"

And there went my mini-vacation.

"Yeah. Sure. Book the flight and send me the info."

I hung up and after a moment of complete silence, burst into laughter. At that moment, Adam Black walked into the shop. He paused, eyed me warily, and cocked his head.

"Everything okay?"

"Everything is just fine. I just got hired to design the furniture for some guy's chalet in

Colorado. I'm leaving tomorrow."

"Holy shit, Logan, that's amazing. Congratulations! Or mazel tov, as my people would say."

He clapped me on the shoulder and gave me a wide smile. Then he bit his lip and looked worried.

"I guess that kind of screws me, though," he said.

"What did you need?"

"I wanted you to design some wine storage for me. When do you think you could manage that?"

I smiled and motioned for him to follow me into the back room. I pointed out some wine racks I'd been working on, using the remains of that reclaimed wood. Adam's eyes widened in delight.

"I'll take them all. Shit, man. This is brilliant."

It was turning out to be a pretty good day.

*

Before I could blink, I was on an airplane headed to the States. The drive out to the airport had been brutal, in the middle of a storm, and I was just relieved the flight had been able to take off as scheduled. I slept most of the way there, having passed out in the middle of a movie that had been way over-hyped.

A driver picked me up at the airport and drove me to my hotel, where I checked in and grabbed a quick shower before heading out to meet the client. Once again, a driver appeared to take me and I got into the car, wondering what I'd gotten myself into.

When I arrived at the "chalet," I discovered it to be a large, sprawling mansion nestled into the mountain. One entire side was made of windows, privacy not being an issue given the seclusion of the property. The architecture was spectacular—majestic but not overstated. I was itching to get inside.

As soon as I stepped out of the car, the front door opened and a leather-clad guy emerged, a few years older than me. He was olive-skinned, with long hair and a road-worn look to him, like he'd been touring with a rock band for ages.

"Hey," he called. "I'm Damien, come on in."

I walked into the house and after removing my coat and boots, took a first look around.

"Holy shit. You're Damien Axe from Hammer of Thor."

He laughed, delighted.

"You heard of us, dude? Awesome."

"You just played Rocky Heights this past summer. I was at the show."

"Get out! That's crazy, man. That was a good show. Next time I'll get you backstage."

I laughed.

"That would fucking kick ass." I started walking around the space, getting a feel for it. "So what exactly is it you're looking for?"

He walked me around the house, pointing out all the areas he wanted to commission pieces for. It would've been crazy for me to build them all at home and ship them out, and I said so.

"What do you suggest?" Damien asked.

I considered it for a moment.

"I could always rent out some space here, source the material locally. It would be the sustainable thing to do, in any case. I mean, look around."

Damien laughed and clapped my back.

"I like you, dude. Yeah, that sounds great. When can you get started?"

I took a deep breath and did the mental math. I would definitely have to hire someone to watch the shop. And Lainey was only in town for another week—I didn't want to lose the opportunity to see her.

"How about this? I'll spend the next couple

of days setting everything up, then I'll go back home and take care of business. I'll be back here next week to get started. Shouldn't take longer than six weeks, two months tops."

Damien reached out and we shook hands. After a brief exchange, I took him up on his offer to borrow his driver and started my search for a workspace. It was only when I was settled into the back of the car and was able to take a deep breath that I realized, for the first time in my life, I'd taken a risk.

CHAPTER SEVENTEEN

Lainey

That first night with my father was a trip. Aside from the obligatory awkward vibe, there was the fact that I knew something he didn't. Something major. But I wasn't ready to show my hand yet.

As soon as he came inside, he admitted he knew exactly who I was and that he'd been following my career the entire time.

"Why?" I asked, genuinely curious.

"I loved your mother, so I guess I loved anything or anyone that belonged to her. I just wanted to keep tabs. But she never once talked about her husband, your father."

I said nothing, terrified to be on such shaky ground so quickly.

"Is he alive?" Colm asked.

I nodded, cautiously.

"Is he in Mountain Valley?"

I thought for less than a second before replying, "Very rarely."

"Are you close?" he pushed.

"No, but I'd like to be."

With that, Colm leaned back in his seat at my kitchen table, sipping on his tea.

"I'd always wanted kids. One of my biggest regrets in life."

"Why didn't you have any?" I asked.

He shrugged and sighed.

"Honestly? After your mom, I just never met anyone else I felt the same way about. I'm an all-or-nothing kind of man."

I nodded at that. We'd talked for about another hour, but it was late and he wanted to get back to his hotel. We'd made plans to meet the next day for lunch at a local favourite roadside diner. It had been around when he was living here thirty-five years ago, and I thought he might appreciate the nostalgia.

*

I was waiting for Colm in my favourite booth at the restaurant the next afternoon when it hit me that I hadn't told Logan any of this yet. I wasn't under any obligation, but given how far down this road he'd traveled with me, I figured he should be the first to know. I texted him, but getting no immediate answer, I shoved my phone in my purse when I saw Colm walk through the front door.

There, in the light of day and in the middle of that crowded diner, it was easy to see why my mother had fallen for him. He had a way about him, carrying himself with a confidence that was appealing to everyone around him. I swear half the heads turned to watch him make his way to my table. He was almost ethereal in his movements, gliding across the floor. He matched perfectly with my mental image of a poet.

"Lainey," he said as he sat down, reaching for a menu.

The air between us was easy, all the awkwardness of the previous night gone. We'd broken the ice without even scratching the surface.

"I hope you slept well," I said.

"I did. The Elway is lovely."

I smiled. The waitress came over and took our orders. I noted he didn't order any meat, so I opted for a bagel with cream cheese and smoked salmon. I didn't want to do anything to offend him, though he struck me as the type to live and let live.

"Lainey, I don't want to sound ungrateful, but you never really told me why you wanted to talk."

I knew it had been coming, and I'd prepared for it.

"Well, when I came here a few weeks ago to write this script, an old friend, Logan, showed up with some boxes from my mom. They contained journals and letters. And they were about you. She'd never mentioned you before, and I was curious."

He nodded, mulling this over.

"I can understand that. I was so sorry to hear she'd died. I had always meant to make my way back out here."

I felt the tears rise in my throat. I bit my lip.

"She would have liked that, I think," I managed.

When I felt I could manage, I looked up and saw a lone tear sliding down his cheek.

"You really loved her," I whispered.

"More than anything. I'd have given up anything for her, but she wouldn't let me. She said if I'd stayed, she'd have left me. What was I to do?"

I nodded. I knew how stubborn my mother could be. I'd lived with her for the first eighteen years of my life. And then she'd done everything in her power to push me out of the nest. She knew I had to leave. She had understood. Now I understood why.

My mother had lived through the same thing twice—saying goodbye to the people she loved most in the world. First Colm, then me. She knew I wouldn't come back, would rarely visit, but she encouraged me to leave anyway because it's what she thought would be best for me, despite Logan, whom she also loved dearly.

The food came and the waitress deposited it silently on the table, sensing the charged atmosphere. She slipped away and we ate silently, each of us digesting each other's confessions. He thought he had the deeper need—to see those journals—but I was the one who needed more, who needed the connection.

By the time we finished eating, my decision was made.

"How long are you in town for?" I asked.

"Until Friday," he said.

It was Wednesday. That gave us less than two full days.

"I can always come back, or you can visit me if you like. But I'm speaking to a class Monday morning and I hate to skip those. I get inspired talking to students."

"No, I get it. It's so great that you came up

here in the first place. It's the last thing I expected." I paused. "Listen, I have to run, but I'd love to see you again later, if possible."

He wiped his mouth with his napkin and nodded eagerly. I folded my own napkin back up into a rectangle and placed it neatly by my plate. Then I reached into my bag and pulled out the first journal. I put it on the table and slid it across to him.

"I think you should read this. Then maybe come by my house tonight? Around six?"

He nodded again, more solemnly this time. He took the journal, turned it over in his hand, then slid it into his messenger bag. I stood up, leaned over, and gave him a kiss on the cheek.

"I'll take care of the bill. I'll see you later."

*

As I left the diner, my phone vibrated in my purse and I pulled it out. Logan.

"Hey," I said. "Where are you?"

"Believe it or not, Colorado."

I stopped short, almost bumping into the person in front of me in the parking lot.

"Excuse me?" I said.

"No problem," said the guy in front of me.

"Colorado," Logan repeated at the same

time.

I smiled absently at the other guy then made my way to the car.

"What are you doing in Colorado?" I asked.

"I got a job. For a rock star. He wants me to design furniture for his chalet in the mountains."

I unlocked my door and slid into the driver's seat.

"Holy shit, Logan. When did this happen?"

"Yesterday."

I was speechless.

"Yesterday? And you what? Got on a plane and flew over there today?"

"Yup."

"On a whim?"

"Crazy, right?"

"Yeah," I said. "Crazy."

"How's everything going over there? Ever hear back from your dad?"

"Yeah, actually I did. I'll tell you all about it when you get home. I gotta go."

I turned off my phone and dropped it into my purse.

Colorado. I should've been happy for him, but I was annoyed. He picked up and left for a job, something he'd never done for me. I shook my head, telling myself to snap out of it. This was only further proof that what we'd had was young love. It was nowhere near as serious as it felt when the two of us were in a room together. No.

I started the car and drove home, bracing myself for the evening ahead.

*

When I answered my door at exactly six o'clock, I found a broken man on the other side. I raced to take him into my arms, hugging him close as I walked him inside. Bella ran circles around us, whining, not liking this scenario one bit.

"I never knew," Colm said between sobs.

"Me, either," I said. "It's not your fault."

"There was no other man?" he asked, incredulous.

"No. She raised me alone. She never once gave me any hint as to who my father might be. She was terrified of tying you down."

Colm pulled away from me and took my face in his hands, looking deep into my eyes.

"You would never have been tying me down. I would have given up everything to be here with you."

He pulled me in towards him again, hugging me until I had no choice but to wrap my arms around his waist and hug him back.

"Please stop crying," I whispered.

He pulled away again and slowly peeled off his coat. He then sat and carefully unlaced his boots. As I watched him, I rubbed my nose, something I always did when I was nervous. When I looked at him, I saw he was doing the same. We locked eyes and laughed.

"I guess I would've figured it out eventually," he said. I just smiled.

He followed me into the kitchen and I pulled out some salads I'd prepared for dinner. He looked around, surveying the spread.

"Looks great," he said.

"Thanks. I'm not really up on the whole vegetarian cuisine, so I did what I could."

"Vegetarian?"

"Yeah. You didn't order bacon this morning, so I figured—"

He burst out laughing.

"I'm the furthest from vegetarian you'll find," he said. "I ate a goat's testicles once when I was in Syria."

I laughed, relieved, and went to the fridge to pull out some sliced salami I had bought a couple of days before.

"Perfect," he said, sitting down.

We started eating and after a few moments, I broke the silence.

"I have the rest of the journals for you to read. You can take them back to the hotel with you if you like."

"I'd like that very much," he said. "Reading that first one was like being with Greta again. It was an almost transcendent experience."

I smiled and pushed the food around on my plate.

"What's wrong?" he asked. "You seem distracted."

I said nothing but offered him another small smile.

"Talk to me," he said. "I'm your father."

I didn't know why that struck me as funny, but it did, and I burst out laughing. He watched me for a moment until it hit him, too, and then joined me in my hysterics. There were tears flowing down both our faces by the time we caught our breath. Bella sat at my feet, staring up at me as if I were nuts.

"Did you bring the dog with you from LA?" he asked, wiping the corner of his eye with his napkin.

"No," I said and told him the story of Bella's rescue.

"Looks like there were a few reasons for your trip up here, besides the script."

"Huh," I said. "I hadn't thought of it that way."

"How's that going, by the way?"

I studied him for a moment, my father, the fellow writer.

"Would you like to read it?" I asked.

His eyes lit up.

"I would love that."

I got up and walked over to my desk to pick up the draft I'd printed that morning. I held onto it tightly; I hadn't let anyone read the finished script yet. Not even Beth. I walked back to him and handed it over. He got up from the table and took a seat on the couch, carefully opening the first page.

I slipped on my jacket and boots, leashed up the dog, and took her out for a walk.

CHAPTER EIGHTEEN
Logan

I was browsing the airport bookshop while waiting for my flight to board. As I thumbed through the volumes, I came upon the collected works of Colm Shepherd. I laughed out loud, then held the book up for no one in particular, as if some stranger would share in my appreciation of the coincidence.

I tucked the book under my arm while I grabbed a bag of chips and a soft drink. I paid for all three at the cash register then headed towards my gate. I still had another half-hour to go, but at least I had reading material.

By the time we touched down, I had read through the collection twice. It was breathtaking. Every single poem was about something different but they all tied together under the theme of lost love. I felt like I'd met a kindred spirit. I stood up and gathered my things, preparing to disembark from the plane. I turned on my phone, checking to see if maybe Lainey had called. I hadn't heard from her since our brief conversation and I felt a chill between us, despite the distance.

I made my way off the plane, skipping the baggage carousel as I only had my carry-on. I went through security and exited into the arrivals area, where families and couples were greeting each other with hugs and kisses. I smiled to myself. I've always liked airports, but it was rare that I was the one arriving home. It struck me that it would have been nice to have someone greet me like that, and then I shook it off and headed for the exit.

That's when I spotted Lainey. She caught my eye at exactly the same moment, and we both stood there in shock. Did she know I was coming back that day? Had she come to pick me up? My heart sped up as I walked slowly towards her. Just as I approached, an elderly man came and took her by the arm. I immediately recognized the face from my book jacket. It was like all the breath had been knocked out of me.

"Lainey?" I said, standing there like an idiot while the two of them looked at me.

"Logan. What are you doing here?"

So much for my fantasy.

"I'm just getting back from Boulder. What are you doing here?"

She smiled broadly.

"I brought my dad to catch his flight home. Colm Shepherd, meet Logan Matthews."

Colm looked steadily between his daughter and me before reaching out his hand to shake mine.

"It's a pleasure, sir. Really. I can't believe you're here." I reached into my bag and pulled out my book. "I just read this on the plane. Twice. It blew me away."

Colm laughed, clearly pleased.

"Well, then, Logan. It's truly a pleasure to meet you, too. I've heard some about you from Lainey. Thank you for bringing her those journals and letters. You helped us find each other."

Lainey smiled up at her father, and I wondered what I'd missed. Obviously a lot. Lainey turned back to me.

"Have you got a ride back to town?" she asked.

I shook my head.

"I was going to hire a car," I lied, figuring I'd text Damien's hired driver to cancel.

She paused for a moment, biting her bottom

149

lip. Decision-making time.

"Why don't you stick around? I'll take you back. Silly to waste the money."

"Sure. That sounds great." I looked around. "But why are you in the arrivals area?"

Lainey and her dad looked at each other and burst out laughing.

"We just got a little confused," she said. "Come, let's find the check-in counter."

We went upstairs and eventually found Colm's airline. He looked in confusion at the kiosks and Lainey gently took his passport from his hand.

"I'll take care of it," she said.

When she walked off towards the machine, Colm turned to me.

"I know how to use the damn machine," he said.

"I figured."

"Lainey didn't tell me a lot, but I sense there's more here than meets the eye. I don't want to mix in, having just arrived on the scene, but let me say this—"

"If I hurt her, you'll kill me."

He laughed, tickled again.

"Do I look like the violent type? No. What I was going to say was in the very short time I've known her, I can tell she's an extraordinary woman. So you must be pretty special yourself.

Given the fact that you're here, and she moved away, I feel like our stories have much in common. Try not to make the same mistakes."

Lainey joined us at that moment, handing Colm his luggage tags and passport. He smiled in thanks and got to work affixing the tags. Lainey shot me a curious glance but I just smiled. We'd have plenty of time to talk later.

*

"How did it happen?" I asked in the car as I texted my other driver.

"Logan, it was crazy. He never replied to my message, and then the next night he just showed up at my door. He didn't even know I was his. Just the fact that I was part of my mother's life was enough to get him on a plane."

"Sounds like something you'd do," I mumbled.

"It does, doesn't it?" She fiddled with the radio. "Doesn't sound like something you'd do, though. What happened with Boulder?"

"Talk about crazy. Damien Axe from Hammer of Thor called me to design his furniture. Can you believe it? I head back next week to do the job."

"You're leaving Mountain Valley? For how long?" she asked.

"Six weeks? Unsure. When do you leave?" I asked, dreading her answer.

"Next week."

"You heading home?" I asked.

"Unsure. I was, but now I'm thinking maybe I'll go to Vancouver and visit Colm. I mean, my dad. So weird." She laughed nervously. "We just clicked, Logan, like we'd known each other forever."

"Or like you were father and daughter."

"Ha. Yeah, that too." She paused for a moment. "What's going to happen with your shop? And your business?"

"I've got to hire someone. I'm going to find out who did the work on your cabin. It's good work. Maybe they're available."

She nodded, then focused her attention on the road. Carly Simon was singing on the radio and she sang along under her breath. I glanced over and saw the ghost of a smile on her lips. There was so much for us to say, but neither of us was talking. At that moment, it was enough to simply be.

An hour later, she pulled up outside my place. She hadn't been over yet. Since discussing the fact I'd bought her mother's house, we'd never really brought it up again.

She sat in the car, staring at it, an unreadable expression on her face.

"Do you want to come in?" I asked.

She bit her lip.

"Bella's waiting for me."

"She'll be fine."

She took a deep breath and let it out slowly. Then she turned to me.

"Just for a few minutes."

CHAPTER NINETEEN

Lainey

I stepped into the house expecting to be transported back in time, but when I looked around, I saw the place looked different. Like, entirely different. He'd knocked down walls and put up new ones. The stucco was replaced by exposed wooden beams. The tiled fireplace was redone in stone. In short, it was magnificent.

"Logan. You did all this?"

I glanced over to find him looking at me, studying my face to gauge my reaction.

"Yeah," he said softly. "What do you think?"

"It's amazing. I mean, it's totally different from my mother's house, but it's beautiful. It's you. It really is."

He sighed in relief and pulled off his coat.

"I'd always loved the bones of this house. I tried to get your mom to make some of these changes, but she was never interested."

"You kept in touch," I said, surprised.

"Yeah. She never told you?"

I shook my head.

"No. We never talked about you."

He looked like I'd shot him in the chest.

"I didn't mean it like that, Logan. It wasn't a conscious thing. At least not on my part, maybe it was on hers. My mother was always focused on my future, not my past. She wasn't one to look back or reminisce."

"Yeah, I guess I get that." He took my coat and hung it up. "Come, let me show you around."

He gave me a tour of the house. It was a two-storey cottage—living room, dining room, and kitchen downstairs with two bedrooms and a den on the upper floor. He'd done a beautiful job, and each and every room looked well lived-in and warm. I paused in the den, where a collection of framed photos sat on a side table. I picked one up and studied it. It was a picture of the two of us, sitting on the grass watching a soccer game in the town square. It was a candid shot, and we were looking at each other and laughing. I hadn't seen the picture in years, and I felt a swell of emotion rise in my chest.

I turned and he was standing right behind me.

"I love that shot," he whispered.

"It's a great picture," I said, putting it back. "I'd forgotten about that day."

I didn't have to turn around to know his hand was hovering somewhere above my shoulder. I could feel the magnetic pull of his body. Every hair on my body was standing up, anticipating his touch. But it didn't come. I finally turned to face him and the expression that greeted me was so forlorn, while at the same time, hopeful.

I reached out and stroked his cheek, feeling the heat spread through my hand and up my arm. How could he still have this effect on me, almost two decades later? He grabbed my wrist and kissed me. It wasn't a light or tentative kiss. It was filled with intent. I pulled away.

"Logan."

"Come on, Lainey, tell me you don't feel it, too. Christ, your goddamn body is calling out for mine."

He moved towards me again and I didn't back away. He reached for me and I just stood there, paralyzed. I wanted him, there was no denying that. And the look in his eyes told me there was no one else for him, nowhere else he wanted to be. I closed my eyes and when I opened them, he was right in front of me again, looking down into my eyes, asking permission.

I tilted my chin upwards, just a bit, but it was enough. His mouth came down over mine, his tongue seeking entry as his hands wove through my hair. My decision made, I tore at his shirt, pulling it over his head as he worked the buttons on my top. Within seconds we were both naked, hands all over each other's bodies. It was complete chaos. He grabbed my wrists and took a step back.

"Stop. Slow down. Come."

He let go of my wrists to take my hand and led me through the hallway to his bedroom. There was a massive king-size bed in a gorgeous mahogany frame, which he'd obviously made himself. I turned to kiss him, and he lifted me easily off the ground as I wrapped my legs around his waist. He walked us over to the bed but didn't set me down, opting to hold me a while longer as he kissed me thoroughly.

I let my fingertips trail across his back, from shoulder to shoulder, as he kissed a path towards my ear. I could feel him growing hard against me and I tightened my legs around him, pulling him in as close as I could.

"You feel amazing," he whispered.

He had his hands on my waist, supporting me, but I unwound my legs and slid down until my feet touched the floor. I ran my hand across his chest, marvelling again at his sculpted abs and muscled shoulders. I met his eyes and found him just waiting for my cue. I let my hand drop, tracing a line across his hip. His hand reached out and cupped the back of my head, gently pulling me in closer as he leaned in for another kiss.

"I have never wanted you more," he said.

I reached down and took him in my hand, stroking him as his breath grew short. I let go, intending to get down on my knees, but he lifted me once again and deposited me on the bed, crawling on top of me and pushing me back on the mattress. I raised my arms above my head and he started a slow descent, kissing my palms, my wrists, my forearms, working his way slowly towards my shoulders.

He continued down my body, pausing at my breasts to pay special attention. By the time he hit my navel, I was writhing on the bed, moaning and begging for him to touch me. He bypassed the important bits entirely as he worked his way down my legs, using his hands to create a path that he followed with his tongue.

158

"Logan, please—"

"Please, what?"

"I want—"

"What do you want, Lainey? Tell me."

He kissed the soles of my feet, rubbing his thumb along my ankle bone, causing sparks of electricity to fly up my legs. Who was this man? Where had he learned all this?

"I want you," I cried.

He rolled over and pulled open the top drawer of the night table, from which he extracted a condom. Without wasting a second, he freed it from its foil wrapper and slid it on, climbing over me once again.

Supporting himself on his elbows, he bent down on kissed me gently on each eyelid before finding my lips. It was something he used to do when we were teenagers and it stirred something deep in me. I wrapped my arms around his neck, losing myself in his kiss. He brought one hand down between us, slipping it between my legs. I moaned into his mouth, grinding up against his hand. He slid one finger, then two, deep inside me and slowly stroked me from the inside.

I broke the kiss, gasping for air. His thumb found my clit and began making small, circular motions as his fingers continued to work inside. He lowered his head, taking my nipple in his mouth. I could feel my orgasm building and I reached down to take him in my hand. As soon as my fingers closed around him, he was on top of me again, guiding himself inside.

He stilled, watching my face as the foreign-yet-familiar feeling of having him inside me took over my body. And then he began to move. Slowly at first, then with increasing speed as his body tensed. He started calling my name, and he reached down between us, his thumb and forefinger pinching my clit until the orgasm exploded in my lower body before fanning out to my extremities. I lay there, shaking and spent as he continued to thrust. I brought my knees up, then wrapped my legs around his waist. Lifting my head off the mattress, I found his nipple and took it in my mouth, swirling my tongue once before beginning to suck.

"Oh, fuck, Lainey!"

His hips snapped against mine and he collapsed against me as he came. I held him close, running my hands up and down his back before coming to rest on his perfect ass. I waited until his breathing returned to normal before giving him a squeeze.

"I can't breathe," I said.

He laughed and rolled off me.

"You're not the 120-pound weakling you

were in high school, you know."

"Hey!" he said. "I resent that. I was never 120 pounds."

I laughed and rolled on my side to face him.

"That was nice," I said.

He reached out to tuck a strand of hair behind my ear.

"It was more than nice," he said. "Was it weird having sex in your mom's house?"

I laughed.

"Nah. We had sex in her last house, right?"

He laughed, too.

"I gotta get home to Bella, though."

I don't know why I said it. It wasn't like I wanted to flee, but part of me wanted to flee. He kept his expression guarded, revealing nothing. I swallowed, for a moment thinking I'd take it back, but I couldn't. I really did need to get out of there.

"Yeah, of course," he said.

He rolled out of bed and pulled a pair of sweats out of a drawer. He put them on then walked to the den to retrieve my clothes. I should say something, anything. I just didn't know what.

He came back into the room and put my clothes on the bed. I couldn't meet his eyes.

"I don't mean to run out," I said.

"Yes, you do. That's your solution for

everything."

I tensed up. That was a low blow. I pulled on my clothes in silence, then stood up and walked out of the room. It was a minute before Logan followed me down the stairs. He finally broke the silence as I pulled on my coat.

"Listen, I don't know what just happened there. Why it keeps happening. Can we not just enjoy each other's company for the week we have left together? Without all the emotional baggage?"

"You're the one who threw the cheap shot," I said.

"Fair."

After another moment of silence, I put out my hand in a peace offering. He shook it, then pulled me in for a hug. I obliged him and when we pulled away, he planted a soft kiss on my lips.

"Will I see you again?" he asked.

"Of course. Bella would be furious if we left without saying goodbye."

CHAPTER TWENTY
Logan

Every time I got close, she pulled away. Each time it hurt a little more, but would I trade that for the time we were spending together? Not a fucking chance.

I spent the next few days getting my shit together. In the end, I opted to hire Desi, Adam's old nanny, to watch the shop for me while I was gone. She had returned to Mountain Valley after college almost two years ago and had been taking odd jobs here and there while figuring out what to do with her life. At twenty-two, it was fine. At twenty-four, she was starting to panic.

She knew nothing about wood, but her only job was to watch the place, take money for sales, and call local contractors for any emergency jobs at the Andersons'. I'd realized I'd have a workshop in Boulder, and if needed, could work on other projects on the side as they came in.

She was a quick study, and I felt pretty confident leaving the place in her hands. She'd come with very high recommendations from Adam, and I hadn't known him to tolerate any bullshit.

I'd secured a room in a house in Boulder with three other guys roughly my age. It would be interesting, but I didn't anticipate spending much time there. I'd also found a sweet workshop I was looking forward to using. A change of scenery was going to be nice.

The only thing left to do was pack up and go. But I wasn't willing to do that before seeing Lainey one more time.

*

"What can I get you?" Bree asked.

I stared at her in shock. I'd been to Cagney's bar many times, but I'd never heard her utter those words. I cocked my head and studied her.

"Why are you asking?"

"Dude, I can't get a read on you tonight. You've said nothing, your expression is void of any human emotion—what's it going to take to cheer you up? OH! Never mind. Got it."

Bree whipped around and started reaching for bottles. I watched as she mixed my drink. She was probably close to thirty, jet black hair that fell past her shoulders, with a tattoo of the moon on the back of her left shoulder and the sun on the front of her right shoulder—both visible with the black tank-top and jeans she was wearing. She was by far the most casually dressed in the place, but it worked for her.

"She's pretty amazing, isn't she?"

I turned to my right and saw a blond woman, around my age, sitting on the stool beside me. She looked vaguely familiar, but I couldn't put a name to her face, which meant she was likely a first-season renter. I smiled at her.

"That she is," I replied.

"What are you drinking?" she asked.

"I have no idea," I laughed.

She smiled in return and signalled for Bree.

"Can you make me one of whatever you're making him?" she asked.

Bree just shook her head.

"Nope, but I'll make you a drink."

"Still think she's amazing?" I asked.

The woman laughed and put out her hand.

"I'm Jessica. You're Logan, right?"

"Yeah," I said, shaking her hand. "Have we met?"

"No, I follow you on Instagram. Your work is beautiful."

"Thank you very much. That just bought you a drink."

Bree came over a couple of minutes later, placing two drinks in front of us. She shot me a dirty look and for the umpteenth time, I cursed living in a small town where everyone knew my business.

There was nothing left for me to do that night, so I asked Jessica if she had plans for dinner. She said no, and accepted my offer graciously. Jen tensely led us to a table and handed us the menus. If Jessica sensed anything, she didn't let on. I, however, was thinking another restaurant might have been a better choice.

*

We were just finishing up dessert when I told Jessica about my upcoming trip. She was easy to talk to, and things just spilled out of me. Somewhere around the main course, she'd

166

started giving me the look, that one that said if I wanted to take her home, I could.

"Hey, having a nice night?"

I looked up and there she was. Lainey was standing right over my shoulder, smiling the sweetest smile I'd ever seen grace her face. But she couldn't hide the pain in her eyes. In that instant, I realized what an idiot I'd been. I was a fool to think I could lose myself in someone else. I smiled up at her.

"Lainey, meet Jessica. Jessica, Lainey. Lain —would you like to join us for dessert? We're almost done, but I'm sure Liam would send something out for you."

She studied me, trying to read me, determine my motivation. I knew her so well, why didn't she know my offer was sincere? I glanced over at Jessica and understood. The ice in her eyes would've sent any other woman away with her tail between her legs, but Lainey was trying to figure out her next move.

"You know what? I'm good. I'm going to grab a drink at the bar. Just handed in my final draft and I need a moment to process."

With that, she disappeared towards the bar. I turned back to Jessica and smiled, but she was having none of it.

"Girlfriend?" she asked.

"Not quite," I answered honestly.

Jessica pulled the napkin off her lap, folded it neatly, and placed it beside her plate. Then, with a tight smile, she stood up and pulled on her jacket.

"Thanks for dinner," she said.

"Jessica, I'm sorry—"

She put up her hand, then turned and walked away. Fair. I deserved that. I signalled to the waiter that I was returning to the bar and walked over to find a seat next to Lainey. She was laughing when I approached but got very quiet as I took my seat.

"I'm sorry, did I ruin your evening?" she asked, not sounding at all sorry.

"You saved it," I said.

"Oh please." She rolled her eyes. "Don't give me that bullshit."

"It's true."

"Why? You're free to do as you please. You don't belong to me."

"My heart does. Don't you fucking see that?"

She took a sip of her drink.

"When do you leave?" she asked.

"Monday."

It was Saturday night. I had planned on going to see her and Bella the next day, but the look in her eyes told me she thought I was going to take off without saying goodbye.

"I never would've done that," I said quietly.

Bree walked over and put a drink down in front of me.

"You don't deserve it. That was a dick move tonight."

I sighed heavily and took the drink, not bothering with a reply. I turned back to Lainey.

"When's your flight?" I asked.

"Tuesday."

"Must be a huge relief, to have handed in the draft," I said.

"Yeah, a day early, too." She laughed without a trace of humour.

"Come on, that was a huge achievement given the problems you were having with it. I thought you said you were celebrating."

"I never said that."

She was right. She hadn't. But why shouldn't she? I signalled Bree for another round of…whatever. She gave me the stink eye but obliged anyway.

"Well, I think we should celebrate," I said, raising my glass and clinking it to her untouched one.

She raised her eyebrow, rubbed her nose, and picked up her drink.

CHAPTER TWENTY-ONE

Lainey

On Sunday morning, I rolled out of bed and wandered into the living room, surveying the scene as I contemplated packing up. I'd lent the journals and letters to Colm, with the promise that he'd ship them to me as soon as he was done. Or maybe even bring them by, he'd hinted. We had a lot of time to make up for and he wasn't wasting any of it.

I'd only stuck around for a couple of drinks with Logan the night before. Anything more than two would have led us back to one of our houses, and I wasn't prepared to go through that again. Instead, I'd opted to come home and start my piles—my favourite method of packing.

I made my way through those piles, mentally

packing them up into my various bags. I'd travelled light, but I'd acquired quite a few things in my short time in Mountain Valley. I knew I'd need another suitcase just for Bella's things.

I turned to look at Bella, who was waiting patiently by the door. I still hadn't sorted out if I was going straight home, or if I was going to make a detour in Vancouver. Either way, I realized that bringing her along was going to be more difficult than I'd anticipated. After taking her for a nice walk, I came back to the house, showered, and headed into town.

My first stop was Franni's. I'd had a genius idea to put in an order for some frozen cinnamon buns, and I figured I'd bake them up as soon as I got to wherever I was going. The bell rang overhead as I walked through the door, and I smiled sadly, knowing it would be the last time I'd hear them for God knew how long.

Tess smiled when I approached the counter and the seed of an idea formed in my head.

"I've got all your stuff for you. Wait here," she said.

She disappeared into the kitchen and returned with several sealed plastic bags containing my frozen treats. I eyed the lot and silently relented that maybe I'd need two extra bags. It was worth it. She placed them on the counter and rang up my bill.

"Looking forward to getting back home?" she asked.

"I am. Although I have to say, this has been a pretty special trip."

"Well, I know I'll miss you."

I smiled at Tess. We'd gotten the chance to hang out a few times and I really enjoyed her company. She was a woman who knew what she wanted.

"Listen, I have to ask you something. Please feel free to say no," I said.

"What is it?"

"I'm thinking it's not the best time to bring Bella with me. That I should figure out where we're going to live first—there's a no pets clause in my lease. Would you mind watching her for a few weeks while I sort it out?"

Tess grinned ear-to-ear.

"Would I mind? I'd love it! Oh my god, Livvy will love it!"

I smiled at that. Livvy was Adam's five-year-old daughter. When they'd met, kids were a hard no for Tess, but she'd confided in me that this one had really grown on her.

"You really love that little girl, don't you?" I asked.

"Like she's my own. I never would've

172

believed it, but life has a way of surprising you. Sometimes, the things you think you don't want are exactly what you need."

I thought about that for a moment, silent as I put the frozen goods in my shopping bag.

"I'll drop Bella off tomorrow, okay?" I asked.

"Perfect. I'm off at six. Anytime after that."

I thanked her again profusely, gathered my loot, and left.

*

After running a few more errands, I returned home to get in as much quality time with Bella as I could. The thought of being without her for even two weeks was breaking my heart, which was crazy because she'd only come into my life a month earlier.

I was just leashing her up for our last long walk through the woods together when the doorbell rang. Already in my coat, I opened the door to find Logan standing out front, two suitcases by his side. My heart dropped. I'd somehow thought we'd end up spending time together that night, but I realized then how foolish that was, to expect to be in his life while constantly pushing him away.

"You off already? I thought you were leaving

tomorrow," I said.

"I am."

We both stood there, staring at each other. I stepped aside and he came into the house, dropping his bags on the floor.

"Were you on your way out?" he asked.

"Just taking Bella for a walk. Want to come?"

He nodded curtly and zipped up his coat. Together, we left the house and headed towards the trailhead at the end of the road. It was Bella's favourite walk, and since it was the last time she'd be doing it, I really wanted to savour it.

We'd been walking for about ten minutes before Logan finally broke the silence.

"I want to spend the night."

I almost stopped to say something but kept walking.

"Lainey, who knows when we'll be together again? I haven't seen you in close to twenty years, dammit. Have you learned nothing from this trip? From us? From your parents? You have to grab hold of what's in front of you with both hands."

This time I did stop. I turned to him.

"And then what? Let it go again?"

"Can't we figure that part out later?"

"When did we switch roles?" I demanded. "I'm the risk-taker, you play it safe. That's the way it's always been."

He just shrugged.

"You're the one who wanted to stay still, now you're running to Boulder, Colorado on the drop of a dime? Who are you even?" I cried.

I had always felt like I had the upper hand in our relationship. Not that it was something I thought about, or ever used to my advantage, but because I was the one who was willing to leave Mountain Valley, I felt like I was the one in control. At that moment, Logan was shattering every illusion of control I'd had. I could no longer predict his next move, guess at his motivations. He seemed to be able to read me just like he had in high school, yet I felt lost without a map. It was unfair.

"Maybe I've grown up. Just give me a fucking chance, Lain."

He took the leash from me and started walking ahead. I let him go for a while, needing a few minutes by myself to process what had just happened. Only a few words had been exchanged, but they were packed with so much meaning and so much history it was almost overwhelming.

I watched the familiar shape of his back as he moved through the woods. Bella kept close to his side, never pulling on the leash or having any desire to stray. I closed my eyes and I could picture him twenty years younger, moving across the football field. My heart filled, and when I opened my eyes again, he was out of sight. I sighed and started walking.

I caught up with them by the side of a frozen stream. Bella kept pawing at it, water flowing around the ice, but she couldn't figure it out. She turned to the snowbank and started eating that instead. Logan let out a laugh.

"She's a clever dog, isn't she?"

"That she is. I'm leaving her with Tess for a couple of weeks."

He looked at me, surprised.

"Why?"

"My lease doesn't allow for pets. I was worried about landing in LA and having nowhere to keep her until I sorted things out. This seemed like the most humane thing to do."

"I'm sorry I'm not here to take care of her."

"Don't be ridiculous."

"Does this mean you'll be coming back for her?" he asked.

"No." I shook my head. "I'll have Tess send her out. It's not like anyone can stay with her on the plane, anyway."

Why were we talking about the dog when there was so much more to be said? I was frustrated, and I need to take control of the situation.

"Logan. What do you have in mind? Seriously."

He bent down and unhooked Bella's leash, letting her wander through the trees. He walked over and took my gloved hands, bringing them up to his chest.

"All I have in mind is you. I just want to be with you. How the fuck did we let so much time pass? How did we let this slip away?"

"You have to stop that. We were kids. It was another lifetime ago."

"But we're not kids anymore. And it's like life handed us a second chance. And then it brought your father along to show us the consequences of not taking that second chance. Don't you see that?"

I sighed.

"Of course I see that. But you still haven't told me. What do you want?"

He dropped my hands and lifted my chin so I was forced to meet his gaze.

"I want you to want me as much as I want you."

"I do," I said without hesitation.

He let out a long breath.

"So let's sit down, share a bottle of wine, and figure this shit out."

His eyes were pleading with me, but I had no intention of turning him down. Standing before me, his heart in his hands, he was offering himself to me once again.

CHAPTER TWENTY-TWO
Logan

As soon as we got back to Lainey's house, I went in search of the bottle of wine. I found a nice white chilling in the fridge and fished the corkscrew out of the drawer.

"I was leaving that for the next renter," she laughed.

"That explains why it was the only thing in the fridge."

I unscrewed the cork while she got two glasses from the cupboard. I followed her back into the living room and after she settled into the couch, I poured the wine before sitting down myself.

"You going to miss it at all?" I asked.

"I am. I really am. Coming home wasn't what I thought it would be."

"Do you wish you'd done it sooner?"

"I wish I'd visited my mom more," she admitted.

I reached out and squeezed her hand.

"But there's something about being here, in the mountains. It's rejuvenating. I don't think I'll stay away so long again." She glanced over at me. "Besides—"

"Besides."

We gazed at each other for a moment until she broke the spell by taking a sip of wine. The energy in the room shifted and if I didn't want this to be just another hook-up, we had to have it out.

"Lainey."

"I know."

"I'm not as opposed to travelling anymore," I offered. It was really my only bargaining chip.

"I'm sure this job will lead to many more like it," she said. "You'll have to get used to the travelling."

"Do you travel a lot?" I asked.

"Some. Not extensively. But I can write from anywhere."

"Lain, I feel like we're dancing around the point here. Do you want to try this? Do you want to see if we can make it work?"

She offered me a weak smile, but I could see

the hope in her eyes. She wanted it, too. She was just scared.

"Tell me," I said. "Whatever it is, you can tell me."

She took a long sip of wine.

"Seventeen years ago, I made the decision to leave Mountain Valley, and you, in search of something else. And I found it. I have a great life and a great career. But until I came back here, until I saw you again, I hadn't realized that a huge part of my life had been missing."

She stood up and started pacing.

"I've dated. I've been with other men. But I never felt for any of them what I felt for you. What I feel for you. But now here we are, and we don't even know if we're the same people anymore, and I'm willing to turn my entire life upside down in order to find a place for you in it."

I said nothing, sensing she wasn't done. She shot me a quick glance, then resumed her pacing.

"I mean, seriously, Logan. We don't even know each other anymore. We're relying on this." She paused in her pacing and motioned to the air between us, the air that was charged with electricity that resulted from simple proximity to each other.

I let that charge pull me in. I stood up and

walked slowly towards her, ignoring her wary expression. I took her face in my hands and kissed her forehead. She closed her eyes and I kissed each eyelid in turn. Then I lay a trail of kisses along her cheek, lifting her chin with my forefinger to cover her mouth with my own.

Bella whined at our feet and I nudged her gently with my toe. She took the hint and took off for the guest room. Lainey pulled away.

"Why is this so good?" she asked.

"Because I love you," I said and kissed her again. "Because I know you."

She wound her arms around my neck and kissed me deeply, letting me know she'd surrendered. I whispered in her ear.

"Let me show you how well I know you."

I lifted her up and carried her into her bedroom. I lowered her to the ground and when she reached for me, I took a step backwards. She looked at me, questioning, and I smiled.

"Take off your clothes," I said.

She stood there and blinked, confused.

"I said, take off your clothes."

Slowly, she started unbuttoning her sweater. She held my gaze as she took it off, then pulled her camisole over her head. I caught myself holding my breath as she unzipped her jeans and peeled them off. She stood there, in her bra and panties, looking at me. I nodded, encouraging her to continue.

"Who are you?" she whispered.

"It's just me. I promise. Now take them off."

She unclasped her bra and my breath caught at the first glimpse of her breasts. She eased off her panties and tossed them to the side. She stood up tall, brushing the hair out of her face as she held my gaze.

"Lie down," I said.

She walked over to the bed and climbed on, making herself comfortable as a playful grin crept across her face. She drew up her knees, planting her feet on the mattress. I laughed softly and shook my head, and she lowered her legs.

I walked over and sat down next to her. I ran my hand over her shin, stopping to trace the scar across the bottom of her left knee.

"First grade. Duck-duck-goose." I bent down and kissed the scar and she laughed, delighted.

I ran my fingertip along the inside of that same knee, just to where it met the beginning of her thigh.

"And the pulled hamstring in seventh grade."

I parted her legs and leaned in to run my tongue along that group of muscles. She gasped and took hold of my head. I nuzzled the back of her thigh before pulling away.

My finger continued its journey up her leg, crossing over to the right leg and pausing to circle a long, thin scar.

"This is new," I said, glancing up at her.

Her eyes were closed, head resting against the pillows.

"Kitchen accident with a knife," she murmured.

"Stupid knife," I said, kissing it.

There was a mole on her right hip that had been there forever. I used to joke it looked like a map of the mainland of Hawaii. It was funny because at the time, I had no idea what that looked like.

"Hawaii," I whispered. She just sighed.

There were new marks on her body, ones I wasn't familiar with but was looking forward to getting to know better. There were years on both of us, but she was no less beautiful than the day I met her. More so.

I leaned over and gave the mole a quick kiss before tracing a line with my tongue across her hip to a tiny scar just below her navel. She moaned, shifting on the bed and running her hand through my hair.

"I will never forget rushing you to the hospital from my seventeenth birthday party, arriving mere moments before your appendix might have erupted."

I gave that scar a serious kiss because it had once given me a serious scare.

"Logan," she sighed.

I looked at her and smiled, then ran my thumb up her side to her breast, cupping it in my hand.

"I can name the year, date, and time that these babies made their appearance. We were going to the movies in June, and you showed up at the theatre in this little tank top and I almost came in my pants."

She burst out laughing and I covered her mouth with mine, quickly returning her to her aroused state. When I felt her melt beneath me, I broke the kiss and returned my attention to those magnificent breasts.

"I don't even remember what movie we saw. The only thing on my mind was getting my hands on these." I ran my hand across one breast, then the other, watching as her eyes fluttered closed.

I dipped my head, taking her nipple in my mouth. I'd yet to touch her, but I lightly skimmed my hand between her legs, feeling the heat come off her. She arched her back to meet my hand, but I pulled away.

"The first hickey I ever gave you was right

around here," I whispered in her ear, just before biting her neck.

"Oh, god, Logan."

She reached for me, bringing her hand up beneath my arm to rest on the back of my shoulder. She pulled me in closer, trying to press herself against me. She was writhing on the bed by this point, but I wasn't done.

I gently pulled her arm away and brushed the hair off her forehead. A small scar right at her hairline was still visible and I smiled sadly.

"The time the boomerang came back," I said. "Who would've thought?"

I bent down and kissed the scar, then tilted her face up towards mine to plant a soft kiss on her mouth. She kissed me back hungrily, wrapping both arms around my neck and clawing at my clothes.

"You made your point," she said. "Please."

I rolled her onto her stomach and my fingers danced across her back. I made a wide circle around a dime-sized scar on her right shoulder blade.

"That med student who wanted to biopsy your birthmark, calling it suspicious. I could've killed him," I said, bending down to kiss it.

I ran the palm of my hand down her back and over her ass, staying there for a while as she started to grind against the mattress.

"You want me?" I asked softly.

"Yes. God, yes."

"As much as I want you?" I said.

"Yes, I told you already, yes."

I stood up and took off my clothes, throwing a condom on the bed. She rolled over onto her back, relief flooding her face. She reached down between her legs, touching herself, unable to wait any longer. I moved quickly, taking her hand away and replacing it with my own.

I lay down next to her on the bed, my hand still inside her, feeling how ready she was for me. I was so fucking hard I thought I'd explode. Everything between us had been so fast and furious up to that point. It was the first time I'd explored her body like that, seen how time had changed her. She was sexier than ever and I wanted her more than I'd ever wanted her before.

Before I knew it, Lainey's hips arched off the bed and her entire body tensed. Her coming had not been my intention, but she'd been so worked up she needed the release. She cried out and clasped my hand, still between her legs, stroking her, as I leaned over to kiss her.

I reached for the condom and as I moved to get on top of her, she put her hand against my chest and grinned wickedly.

"Not so fast," she said.

CHAPTER TWENTY-THREE

Lainey

"Excuse me?" he said, clearly confused.

"Two can play this game, you know," I said, giving him my best shit-eating grin.

I pushed him back against the bed and straddled him, taking care not to go anywhere near the admittedly impressive erection he was sporting. I leaned over, letting my breasts brush against his chest as I ran my thumb across his left eyebrow, the perfect line of which was broken in two by a crescent-shaped scar.

"Three stitches from the time you fought a guy in a bar for my honour," I said, smiling at the memory.

"You weren't smiling about it then," he laughed.

I bent over and kissed his eyebrow, then his nose.

"Broken nose, senior year football game," I said.

"Worth it. We won that game."

I rolled my eyes and ran my hands across his chest. There was an unfamiliar mark across his shoulder I hadn't noticed before. I looked at him, my eyes asking the unspoken question.

"I was in a car accident in my twenties. I was fine. The mark is from the seat belt saving my life. It's a constant reminder."

I laid my forehead against his chest as I traced the mark with my fingertip, unseen. It was slightly raised, and I could picture its redness behind my closed eyes. It was as if I was searing this new part of him into my memory, my sensory bank.

He ran his hands down my back and I lifted my head. Back to work. I ran one hand along his left shoulder, letting my fingers trace the outlines of his well-defined muscles. I took hold of his forearm and looked him in the eye.

"Broken arm. Junior year. Not football-related. You fell off the couch while we were making out."

His eyes lit up at the memory and he flexed the arm.

"Good as new," he said.

Then he used that arm to flip me over, pinning me to the bed.

"I think you've had your fun," he said, reaching for the condom.

I closed my eyes and raised my hips in response. I reached down and took him in my hand, just the feel of him making me wet, making me anxious to feel him inside me. He gently removed my hand to slide the condom on, then bent down to kiss me as he guided himself in.

His head dropped to my shoulder as he stayed there, motionless, letting the sensation overtake us. He began to move, shifting his hips at an upward angle. I raised my legs, wrapping them around his waist and locking my ankles together. He was so deep inside me but I wanted more. I wanted him to consume me.

As if reading my mind, he reached for my legs and unwound them, bringing my ankles up onto his shoulders.

"Oh, fuck yeah," I cried.

Tenderness and nostalgia out the window, Logan fucked me. Hard. It was a side of him I'd never seen before. There was a fire in his eyes and for the first time, I realized I was looking at Logan the man, not the boy I'd dated in high school. And this man was taking control.

He took my arms and raised them above my head, holding my wrists together with one hand while he supported himself with the other. I was completely powerless, and the heat tore through my body, lighting me on fire.

"Logan—"

I dug my heels into his shoulders and he just drove into me harder, but he slowed his pace, pulling almost all the way out, pausing, and then thrusting back in. I screamed so loud Bella barked from the other room.

"Oh my god," I moaned.

"You going to come for me, Lainey?" he growled.

I was panting, unable to control the waves of pleasure flowing through my body.

"Come for me, Lainey," he commanded.

I was so exposed in this position, so vulnerable. He shifted his hips so that the pressure against my clit was direct and intense and within seconds I exploded into a blinding orgasm. I dropped my feet to the bed, still taking him in deep as he let go of my wrists to brace himself against the mattress as he came. When we were both done, he collapsed on top of me, his hands lost in my hair, breath hot on my neck.

"Only you, Lainey. It's only ever been you."

*

Logan spent the night and while we didn't get much rest, I don't think either of us had any regrets. He left early in the morning after one last walk with Bella. I had a feeling he was going to miss her almost as much as I was. By the time he got back, I'd brewed some coffee and scrambled a couple of eggs. We had a quick breakfast before his car showed up to take him to the airport. It wasn't even eight o'clock when the door closed behind him.

We'd avoided having a real conversation. I'd have loved to blame him for that, but we were both at fault. We were far too wrapped up in each other's bodies to be concerned with anything that might have been on our minds. It was a conscious, but unspoken, decision on both our parts to let it go.

Yet after he left, I felt we weren't done. I almost ran after him but realized there was no point. I knew how he felt. I was the one holding back. And I was going to have to be the one to come forward with some concessions. Did I have to be in LA full-time? Did I want to be a bi-coastal, dual citizen? It had taken so long to build up my present life and I realized one wrong move could destroy it.

That evening, I packed up Bella's things and loaded them, along with her, into the car. I drove to Tess's place, a cute little coach house beside a large estate. As soon as I cut the engine, Livvy came out of the house, sans jacket, racing towards the car. I quickly got out and opened the back door for Bella, who jumped into the snow and ran to greet Livvy.

The two of them tumbled around together as Adam came to the door, holding Livvy's coat with a resigned look on his face, while Tess laughed at his side.

"Livvy! Put on your jacket!" he called.

"Bella, inside," I said.

The dog looked up at me, then trotted into the house. Livvy followed behind.

"Thank you," Adam said, throwing me an appreciative glance.

Tess walked out to the car and helped me unload all Bella's stuff.

"I may have gone overboard. I've never had a dog before. I dunno."

"Don't worry," Tess said, putting a hand on my shoulder. "It's going to be fine."

She reached into the back of the car and pulled out one of three dog beds and a bag of food.

"If you change the food, you just have to do a gradual switch, you know—"

"Lainey. Relax. It will be fine. You will work this out, you will send for Bella."

I nodded. She was right. I was being silly. Two weeks was nothing. And I knew I could sort things out in LA in that time.

We carried the stuff into her house and I could see that Bella had already made herself at home, splayed out across the living room floor on her back with Livvy and Adam both rubbing her belly. Tess laughed then turned to me.

"You have a safe flight tomorrow. Call me when you land."

I nodded and she leaned in to give me a hug.

"I will miss you," she whispered.

"I'll miss you, too."

*

From Tess's, I went to meet Katie for a late dinner. We'd opted for the roadside diner we both loved. I ordered a double bacon cheeseburger, knowing I'd never eat that way back home. There was an image to maintain, of salads and smoothies and early morning hikes in the mountains. Sinking my teeth into that burger, I started to question some of my life choices.

"You look like you're in heaven," Katie said, smiling.

"I think I am."

"You make your decision yet?"

For a moment, I thought she was talking about Logan, but then I realized she just wanted to know which flight I was getting on the next day.

"Yeah. I'm going home. I need to regroup. There's plenty of time to see my dad. We're both on the same coast, and it's an easy trip for both of us. I need to sort out some living arrangements. Anything else would be irresponsible. I want Bella with me."

"I get it." She dipped a fry in ketchup before popping it in her mouth. "Any news from Logan?"

"Yeah. He landed. He's home, settling in with his new roommates. He sent me an address. Maybe he's worried he'll vanish without a trace."

"Maybe he wants you to visit."

I said nothing, polishing off the remains of my burger and taking a sip of my soft drink. Not my diet soft drink, thank you very much. I sighed with pleasure.

"What's with the food high?" Katie asked.

"Last licks. I don't eat like this at home."

She nodded, then shrugged her shoulders. "I mean, I don't eat like this every day, but I think it's essential in the winter months to ensure you're carrying some extra padding."

She raised her soft drink and I raised mine. We clinked glasses and laughed before taking a sip.

"I'm going to miss you," she said.

"Me, too."

Why did it suddenly feel like I was leaving home?

CHAPTER TWENTY-FOUR

Logan

"Do you play poker?" Damien asked.

I was walking around the great room, taking measurements. I stopped at his question and thought about it.

"Well, I've played. I'm not great or anything."

"I'm hosting a game Thursday night. You should come."

"What's the buy-in?" I asked.

"Two large."

I almost choked. I didn't have that kind of money to throw around on a game I could barely play.

"I'd love to, but that's a little rich for my blood."

Damien eyed me for a moment. I tried not to

look at him. He'd come out in his towel and not much was left to the imagination.

"Tell you what," he said. "I'll stake you and you'll pay off your losses in work hours."

Now that was interesting. I wasn't about to hand over two thousand dollars, but for the chance to sit in on a poker game with rock stars, I was willing to provide some free labour.

"Deal," I said.

He grinned and turned to leave the room, whipping off the towel and throwing it at me as he walked away.

"Here, you can sell that on eBay."

I just laughed and turned away as the towel fell to the floor.

*

"Get the fuck out. You're playing poker with Damien Axe?" Steve, one of my roommates, was staring at me with naked disbelief.

"Yup," I said.

Ethan, my other roommate, walked into the room and snorted.

"Please. You're being played. The man is a professional poker player. You cannot beat him, and I'm pretty sure you can't beat anyone else at that table. And that's without knowing you and without knowing anyone else at that table."

I laughed.

"Thanks for the vote of confidence," I said.

"How much is this costing you?" Steve asked.

"Nothing up front, actually. I'm going to pay out my losses in labour." I was very pleased with this arrangement.

"And there we go," Ethan said.

"What does that mean?" I asked.

"I mean, that's his angle. He doesn't want to pay you your full contract, so he's going to beat the pants off you at poker to reduce the cost of his job."

I thought about it for less than a second. The motherfucker was right.

"Well, what do I do? I can't beat him, and I sure as shit can't back out."

Ethan shrugged.

"Set a limit. How much is the experience worth to you? How much are you willing to pay for it? Figure that out, and once you lose that much, get out of the game."

Steve looked up from his sandwich.

"That's actually some pretty solid advice," he said.

"Fuck off, Steve."

"Come on, Ethan. We've been living

together for four years and I've never heard you say something so profound."

Ethan rolled his eyes and mouthed *asshole* to me. I stifled a laugh. I actually liked both of them. I didn't have to worry about their history or annoying habits. My stay was temporary. I could just sit back and relax.

My third roommate, Phil, was away at a conference. He wasn't due back for another week, and I'd yet to meet him. But unless he was a complete jerk, it looked like I'd won the jackpot in terms of housemates.

*

I tried getting in touch with Lainey a few times, but between both our travel schedules over a forty-eight-hour period, it was near impossible. We connected once and I managed to let her know everything was great and passed on my coordinates.

I'd arranged for deliveries on Wednesday, so when I went into my workshop on Thursday morning, everything was ready to go. I inhaled deeply, loving the smell of wood before I got to it, and then loving the smell afterward, too. My entire job was a sensory experience, from the smells to the feel to the sound, and of course—

the sight of the finished product.

It struck me as funny that someone like Damien was into my work. He made no demands on the design, leaving it all up to me and approving all my drawings. For someone with a reputation as an extreme bad boy, he was incredibly easy to get along with.

I tried texting Lainey again, but got no reply. I was starting to get concerned as she was long home by now. There was no reason for her not to return my texts. Unless she'd had a change of heart. But I was so sick of doubting and second-guessing that I decided to put a pin in the whole thing and wait until she decided to come to me. Then I'd know for sure.

CHAPTER TWENTY-FIVE

Lainey

I was home for exactly fourteen hours before I knew what I wanted to do. I had lain awake most of the night, tossing and turning, knowing in my gut that something wasn't right. I'd made the wrong choice, and I wasn't where I was supposed to be.

My contract was done. I was between projects. There was nowhere I *had* to be, so why had I chosen to come home instead of going to Vancouver? Was it really all about Bella? I had, at my fingertips, the chance to resolve all the issues of my past, tie up all the loose ends. Yet there I was, lying in my bed in LA, listening to traffic drive down a filthy street on what was surely another hot day.

I had a meeting with Beth scheduled for ten-thirty. I checked my phone and saw it was already eight o'clock. I allowed myself one final stretch before admitting defeat, silently resigned to spend the day in a state of complete exhaustion.

I showered, ate, got ready, and got my car out of the parking garage for the first time in over a month. I arrived at Beth's office fifteen minutes early, but her assistant shooed me in, insisting she had nothing else on her agenda.

"Elena Wise," Beth announced as I walked through the door.

I stood up a little straighter, automatically transitioning into the persona that name demanded—the successful Hollywood screenwriter.

"Beth, it's so good to see you." I walked over to give her a fake hug and an air kiss. I liked Beth. A lot. She'd been my agent since I arrived and she'd never steered me wrong. We'd developed a close working relationship over the years, and I admired and respected her. But there was no getting around the fact that she was pure Hollywood. She bought into it all. I was just grateful she understood that I didn't.

"Elena, I have to tell you, I got a call from Mason the other day and they are so thrilled. They're deep in casting already and production is due to start in just a few months' time. He wants to know if you'd consider being there for the shoot? On-set revisions? I know it's not the norm, but he's offering good money."

I smiled.

"Let me think about it."

"Of course, of course. Sit. Let's talk about the next steps."

I laughed.

"No rest for the wicked, is there?"

"No commission, either." Beth flashed a brilliant smile and once again I was forced to admire her honesty.

"What have you got?" I asked.

"What have you got?" she countered.

"Honestly? Nothing at the moment. I've been toying with a few ideas, but nothing solid enough to pitch."

She nodded curtly and pulled out a stack of scripts.

"These are all rewrites. Producers have requested you specifically. I think until we land your next project, you should consider taking on a few of these."

I eyed her.

"You worried about me becoming irrelevant?" I asked.

"Not in the least. I want you to make these better movies. I vetted them. They're all fantastic stories, they just need your touch. Trust me. Take a look."

I took the pile and glanced through it.

"And these are a done deal? Any ones I want are mine?"

She nodded.

"So...there's no reason I have to work from LA?"

At that, Beth put down her phone and looked me straight in the eye.

"What aren't you telling me?"

"Nothing. Really. It's just, a few things changed over the past month."

"As is wont to happen when one returns to their hometown. Tell me."

"I met my dad."

Beth and I were not friends. She knew little of my history. But that statement was telling enough, and she understood the enormity of it immediately.

"I see. You want to spend some time with him."

"I do."

She nodded again.

"I don't think that should be a problem."

I stood up and smiled, gathering the pile and placing them in a bag I had stashed in my purse.

"I'll take a look through these and get back to

you."

Beth stood and put out her hand. I laughed, shaking it, and wished her a good afternoon.

*

As the plane touched down in Boulder, I reached for my bag and turned on my phone. Logan had texted, but I paused before replying. I'd already come so far. I thought at that point I should just surprise him.

I'd spoken to my father the night before and told him the whole story. I was so worried returning to Logan would mean going backwards, but he pointed out that I had already achieved what I'd set out to achieve, that this was a new goal, not giving up on an old one. The fact that it was righting a past wrong was the icing on the cake.

Listening to him, I realized how much he missed my mom. Maybe even as much as I did. I understood why she did what she did. Well, most of it, anyway, but I couldn't help but think that Colm might have made different choices, and the world wouldn't have truly suffered for it. It might have been a little less beautiful, but my own family would have been whole.

He ended up telling me what I'd known all along. That I wanted to get on the plane to Boulder. That I wanted to start a life with Logan. That my career was no longer going to bring the kind of happiness it once did, now that I knew this was out there, waiting for me. And I could have both.

I found my way to baggage claim. I had only one bag, but it was too big to pass for a carry-on. As I waited for the luggage to come down the chute, I started getting nervous. It wasn't that I doubted my decision to come; I was just worried about the whole idea of a surprise. Would he be happy to see me? Would I be interrupting his work? Was he going to be in the mindset to have this conversation while in the midst of the most important job of his career?

I saw my purple suitcase come tumbling down onto the conveyor belt and moved in to grab it. Not bothering with a cart, I pulled out the handle and wheeled it through security to the arrivals lounge. I'd rented a car and was anxious to get out of the airport.

I punched Logan's address into the GPS and started driving. I turned the radio on, finding a good classic rock station, then cranking the volume up loud. I needed something to drown out the voices in my head, and Bruce

Springsteen's voice was a damn good option.

I sang along with The Boss as I wove through the snow-dusted roads of Boulder. It was a beautiful city. The sun was just setting and everything had a majestic look to it. The mountains rising up in the background, the low-hanging clouds moving rapidly across the sky. I'd have pulled over to just sit and watch, but my mind was definitely elsewhere.

After about half an hour, I pulled up next to a rambling old house with a large porch. I killed the engine and got out of the car. I left my bag, wanting to take this slowly. It would be good to gauge his reaction before assuming I was spending the night.

It was a Thursday, close to seven o'clock, and I hoped he'd be home. Where else would he be? He'd been in town less than a week, and I imagined he must be exhausted after the abrupt uprooting and starting a new job. I walked up to the front door and, not finding a doorbell, knocked as loud as I could. I heard two voices calling back and forth before footsteps approached. The door flew open and behind it stood a man in his thirties, sporting only sweatpants and a towel around his shoulders. His hair was wet.

As soon as he saw me, he smiled and stepped aside.

"I have no idea who you are, but come on in," he said.

I laughed despite myself. He was charming.

"I'm Ethan," he said. "And you are?"

"Looking for Logan, actually."

"Ah. Of course. The hot ones never come for me."

I looked him up and down, appraising his considerable frame, his curly blond hair, and clear blue eyes.

"Somehow I doubt that," I said.

He burst out laughing and ushered me inside.

"Logan's out," he said. "I'm actually not sure when he'll be back. Do you want me to call him or something? Was he expecting you?"

I shook my head.

"No, that's okay. I'll go. Why don't you just tell him Lainey came by."

His mouth dropped open.

"Lainey? The Lainey?"

I was equally shocked.

"He's mentioned me?"

He burst out laughing just as a second guy came into the room. Tall, dark, definitely handsome. He walked right over and put out his hand.

"Hey there. I'm Steve."

"Forget it, Steve," Ethan choked. "That's

Lainey."

Steve drew his hand back like I was on fire.

"The Lainey?"

"Wow, guys, I don't know what to say." Truly, I didn't. Were they pulling my leg?

"Listen," Ethan said. "He's actually going to be a while. He's playing poker at Damien Axe's place tonight."

"Logan Matthews is playing poker with Damien Axe?" This was surprising.

Ethan nodded.

"Yup. Who knows how late those games go? Why don't you drive over there? I know he'd love to see you. Maybe you'll bring him some luck."

He and Steve burst out laughing, clearly at some private joke.

"I don't think that's a great idea. Just ask him to call me."

"As you wish. But if you change your mind, he lives at the top of Lake Road. No address needed. You'll figure it out."

I thanked them and walked out the door, heading back to the car. I turned the key in the engine and leaned my forehead against the steering wheel. Where was I to go? Drive downtown and rent a hotel room? Find a bar or diner to hang out at until I heard from Logan? Pulling out into the road, I gave my

phone instructions to take me to the top of
Lake Road.

CHAPTER TWENTY-SIX
Logan

I walked into Damien's house and almost burst out laughing at the cliché scene laid out before me. Five guys, all with long hair and tattoos, were sitting around a large poker table in a smoke-filled room. A scantily-clad bartender was mixing drinks behind the bar while some more scantily-clad women roamed the room and chatted with the guys.

What had I gotten myself into?

"Logan! Dude! Come, join us."

I walked over to Damien and took a seat at the table. I ran my hand along the edge of the worn table, noticing the spaces carved out for chips and the felt surface for dealing.

"Admiring my table?" Damien asked with a grin.

"Thinking I could make you a better one."

"Oh! Burn!" one of the guys yelled, laughing.

"I like the way you think, Wood Man," Damien said. "Let's deal you in."

Another guy at the table passed me over my chips and explained the denominations to me. I organized my stack and waited for the croupier to deal the cards. She, of course, was also scantily clad. I'd played a little poker over the years, but I was way out of my league here.

"What can I get you?"

I looked up over my right shoulder where I found a woman in her twenties wearing a crop top and mini skirt. She offered me a sweet smile.

"Beer?" I said.

She turned on her heel and disappeared to the bar. I turned back to the table and threw in my ante before taking a peek at the cards. A minute later, the woman was back with my beer. She put it down beside me but made no move to leave.

I had a decent hand, and I stayed in. I lost, but it wasn't a huge pot and it wasn't enough to shatter my confidence. Yet. I anted up again and waited for the dealer to toss me my cards.

"Do you play?" the woman asked.

"Sometimes," I said honestly.

She leaned over and whispered in my ear.

"I'm Ashley. How about I be your good luck charm for the night?"

I shifted in my chair. I didn't want to be rude, but I also didn't want to give her the wrong impression.

"I'm really just here to play cards," I said.

She smiled.

"We'll see."

She walked away and it was impossible not to look as her ass moved across the room. Yet I wasn't even tempted. I reached for my phone to see if Lainey had called, then remembered I'd surrendered it upon walking in the house.

I played the next few hands, winning two and losing three. I was getting more confident when Ashley came back to join me. She brought me another beer and made herself comfortable on my knee. I stiffened, and Damien shot me an evil grin across the table.

"Having fun?" he asked.

"Absolutely," I said.

Ashley slung her arm around my shoulder as I looked at my cards. She was making me very uncomfortable and I didn't know how to turn this situation around without insulting her or my hosts. Every other guy at the table had a girl on his knee but none of them were having the existential crisis I was.

The guy on my left handed me a cigar and I accepted it graciously. I stuck it in my mouth and Ashley produced a lighter. This woman was really on top of things. It occurred to me for the first time that she might be working. I glanced around the table and realized *all* these women were working.

"Listen," I said to her as a new hand was being dealt. "You're really great and everything, but I'm actually seeing someone."

"Really?" Ashley said. "I don't see her anywhere."

"I'm right here."

Every head at the table whipped around to the doorway, where Lainey stood, hair wet from the snow, a look of absolute pain in her eyes. My heart fucking dropped. She had a knack for showing up just at the wrong time.

I stood up so fast Ashley fell to the floor. Damien burst out laughing. I bent down immediately, offering Ashley a hand, which she ignored as she stood up and dusted off her skirt.

I went after Lainey, who'd already turned around and was heading for the exit.

"Lainey!" I called.

"Logan, dude! You can't leave the table. You're up."

I stood there, frozen, looking from the poker

table to Lainey's retreating form. I took a deep breath then walked over to Damien.

"I will be back. I promise. Give me a few hands. We're talking about true love here."

"Fuuuuck," one of the guys said. "That's heavy. We write songs about that shit."

Damien laughed and waved me off.

"You've got twenty minutes," he said.

I flew out of the room.

*

I caught up with Lainey in the hallway leading to the entrance. Another minute I'd have lost her. I grabbed her by the wrist and pulled her towards me.

"Where are you going?" I asked.

"Clearly you were having a great time. Don't want to ruin your fun."

"Goddammit, Lainey, you heard me tell her I had a girlfriend."

She stopped and closed her eyes, taking a deep breath.

"I got on a plane and I came to find you. And find you I did."

I took her face in my hands.

"You took a risk. Lainey is back."

That got a small smile.

"I'm happy you came," I said.

She said nothing, so I bent down to kiss her. She resisted at first, but I won her over. The minute her arms came up around my neck I knew I had her. I deepened the kiss and she responded, making small noises in her throat as I ran my hands through her hair.

I pulled back, glancing around at our less than private location. I took her hand and led her back into the house. I opened a random door and found the bathroom. Pulling her inside, I shut the door behind us.

"You came back for me," I said.

"I did."

"She's no one," I said.

"I know."

"I mean, I think she's even being paid."

"Yes, Logan, she's being paid."

Lainey couldn't resist laughing at that. She'd always found my innocence so hysterical.

I wrapped my hand around the back of her head and brought her towards me, bringing my mouth down on hers. She pushed me up against the wall and started working the buttons on my shirt. From that moment, everything else was a blur. We went at each other frantically, tearing each other's clothes off.

She ran her hands over my chest and I

reciprocated, holding the weight of her breasts in my hands. Her fingertips trailed down my sides and she dropped to her knees. I closed my eyes, leaning back against the wall. She took me in her mouth and I saw stars. I wound my fingers through her hair, groaning as she took me in deeper.

"Stop, stop," I said.

I leaned over and grabbed her shoulders, pulling her up and kissing her thoroughly. I found her ass with my hands and lifted her gently, prompting her to wrap her legs around me as I turned around and placed her on the edge of the vanity.

I bent my head, taking one nipple in my mouth, then the other.

"Logan," she moaned. It was all the encouragement I needed.

I spread her thighs with my hands as I dipped my head and took a taste. Her hips came up off the counter and she bit her lip to stifle her cries. I worked my hand up her thigh, eventually sliding my thumb inside. She was so wet, so aroused it was driving me insane. I took her clit in my mouth, sucking while gently applying pressure with my tongue.

"Oh, fuck," she cried as she came, laughter bursting forth from the great room down the hall.

I stood up and looked around frantically.

"He's a rock star. There must be a condom in here somewhere."

Lainey put her hand on my arm.

"I'm on the pill, Logan. I'm assuming you're not sleeping around?"

"Not a fucking chance," I said.

I grabbed her hips and brought her to the edge of the counter. She braced her hands on the edge as I guided myself in. She felt so fucking good. We had never had sex without a condom before and the sensation was completely overpowering.

I started moving and she rested one hand on my shoulder. She lay her head back against the mirror and I watched her as I thrust harder and harder, increasing my speed until she was panting. She put her other hand on my chest, letting it trail down until she reached the spot where our bodies joined. She ran her forefinger along my shaft as I went in and out, her thumb rubbing her clit.

Once more her hips raised off the vanity as she approached orgasm. I grabbed her ass with both hands and drove into her, watching her touch herself as she flew over the edge.

"FUCK!" I screamed as I came inside her. I pulled her towards me and her head fell onto my shoulder, her beating heart slamming against my chest.

"Keep it down in there!" Damien yelled from the other room, and once again, laughter.

"I can't show my face out there," Lainey said.

"Then we've got a problem," I laughed. "Because I've still got to play more poker."

CHAPTER TWENTY-SEVEN

Lainey

Too many hours later, Logan and I exited Damien's house. We both reeked of cigar smoke and he was down a couple of thousand dollars, but neither of us could wipe the smiles from our faces.

"Is your car here?" I asked.

"No, Damien sent a driver over for me."

"Well, that was wise. You've certainly had too much to drive. Come on, my rental is down there."

We walked down the curved drive towards the car and he reached for my hand, forcing me to stop.

"I'm so glad you're here, Lainey."

"Me, too."

He kissed me lightly on the mouth, the beer

and cigar smoke coming off him in waves. I was glad we'd had our moment in the bathroom because in his state, I was pretty sure I wasn't getting any more action that night.

I got him into the car and strapped him in. He smiled at me with this goofy look on his face and my heart melted. How could I have stayed away? I walked around to the driver's side, got in, and started the engine.

We were a few minutes into the drive before he spoke up.

"You know, a few years ago, I was having sex with this woman and I called your name."

I had thought he was sleeping, and the admission both startled me and made me laugh out loud.

"What happened?"

"She was pretty pissed."

"After all these years, you were still calling my name?" I asked.

"In my sleep, too," he murmured, his eyes closing.

I turned my attention back to the road. Of course, I'd thought of Logan over the years, but certainly not to the extent I'd have been calling his name out during sex. It made me think about my parents, and the tragedy of what had happened there. I reached over and squeezed Logan's hand, determined not to make the same mistakes.

"Then there was the time I got really drunk after your first movie premiered. I think I called your house a hundred times that night, hanging up each time I heard your voice."

I almost slammed on the brakes.

"That was you?" I yelled. "Jesus Christ, Logan, that scared me to death. That was what, ten, twelve years ago? I remember that like it was yesterday."

He giggled.

"I'm sorry. I couldn't bring myself to say anything. Each time I meant to talk, I swear."

He was certainly being chatty.

"Do you remember Brenda Lawson?" I asked.

Brenda had been in school with us and had had a huge crush on Logan from sophomore to senior year. She did everything in her power to split us up—anything to get her chance with Logan.

"Of course I remember Brenda."

"Whatever happened to her?" I asked.

"She moved away a couple of years ago. To Toronto, I think."

"She ever marry?"

"Not that I know of."

"Did you ever see her again?" I asked.

"Yup. We dated pretty seriously for a couple

of years."

That time I did slam on the brakes. Luckily, it was three o'clock in the morning and the streets were deserted. I sucked in a deep breath and counted to ten before turning to him.

"You dated Brenda Lawson?"

"Yeah."

"You had sex with Brenda Lawson?"

He grinned.

"Yeah."

Every muscle in my body clenched. I was seeing red.

"Your cock was in that bitch's cunt?"

The smile vanished from his face and for a moment his eyes cleared. He seemed to realize he'd made a mistake, and I could see wheels turning in his head as he thought back on the conversation.

"Oh, right. You had some trouble with her in high school, didn't you?"

"Motherfucker," I muttered under my breath as I shifted my foot back to the gas. Perhaps a little too forcefully.

"Lainey," he moaned. "It's always been you."

"Except for the 'couple of years,' it was Brenda Lawson."

"How can you be jealous about this? You didn't date anyone in the past seventeen years?"

"Not Brenda Lawson."

"Well of course not Brenda Lawson."

"Or Jake Cassidy."

That shut him up. Jake Cassidy had spent senior year pursuing me, and when it was clear Logan wasn't following me out of Mountain Valley, he'd offered to come along with me.

"Is that the equivalent?" he asked quietly.

"Yes, that's the damn equivalent."

He heaved a heavy sigh and closed his eyes, leaning back against the headrest.

"Shit, I'm sorry."

We drove in silence the rest of the way home. I wondered if that small victory had been worth poisoning the air between us, or if it had even been a victory at all. I'd wondered about Brenda Lawson for over a decade, but I never had the balls to ask my mother if they'd hooked up. I had never truly wanted to know, fully aware of how much it would hurt. Yet there I was.

I parked outside Logan's house and we both got out of the car.

"Don't you have any luggage?" he asked.

"I do."

"So? Let's grab it," he said.

I swallowed.

"What's wrong?" he asked.

"Do you want me to stay here?"

He blinked and looked at me like I was an imbecile.

"Where's your fucking bag?"

I hit the button on the car remote and the trunk popped up. Logan walked over, retrieved my bag, then headed to the front door. He worked his key in the lock and, despite the ridiculous hour, Steve and Ethan were both sitting in the living room, watching a horror movie.

"Hey, Logan, she found you!" Ethan said.

I smiled.

"That I did."

"How was the game?" Steve asked.

"Actually, it was pretty fucking fantastic," Logan said, grinning at me. I couldn't help it. I smiled back. The fool.

"You win?" Ethan asked.

"Nope, lost every penny."

He took my hand and led me to the bedroom.

*

I got Logan undressed and into bed and before I managed to turn off the light he was out cold. I sat down on the edge of the mattress and took a few minutes to process the past few hours. I'd jumped on a plane to surprise him, caught him with another woman, fucked him like an animal in a rock star's bathroom, then tucked him into bed like a child. It was a lot.

We'd hardly exchanged three sentences during that entire time, aside from his drunken chattering in the car ride home. And that hadn't done anything to facilitate the conversation that lay ahead.

I got up and made my way back to the kitchen, bumping into Ethan who was raiding the fridge.

"Does no one sleep around here?" I asked.

He smiled and offered me a seltzer. I shook my head politely.

"Steve and I are gamers. We're up late. Your boy seems to be on a regular schedule, from what I can tell. It's only been a couple of days."

"I hope you don't mind me crashing here for a bit," I said.

He shook his head and took a swig of his drink.

"Not at all. The more the merrier." He polished off the can and tossed it into the recycling bin. "I'm off to bed. Have a good night—"

"Lainey."

"Right. How could I forget?"

228

CHAPTER TWENTY-EIGHT
Logan

I was awake, but I made the deliberate decision not to open my eyes. Nothing good was waiting for me in the real world. My head was pounding and I could see the bright light streaming into the room against my closed lids. I brought my hand up to my temple to see if there was any physical damage. I wouldn't have been surprised.

I brought my pillow up over my face and tried to piece together the previous night. I knew I'd drank too much and smoked a few cigars. I also knew I lost a lot of money and somehow owed Damien a poker table for the pleasure. I groaned, wondering how long that was going to take me and whether I'd at least been smart enough to insist he pay for materials.

As I mentally went through the evening, more pieces started falling into place. I remembered Ashley on my knee and Lainey's voice —

Holy shit.

I threw the pillow across the floor and opened my eyes, rolling over onto my side to find Lainey, sleeping sounding, blankets pulled up to her chin. A feeling of absolute peace washed over me, my headache was gone, and relief flooded my senses. She was there, in my bed, right beside me. It hadn't been a drunken hallucination.

I carefully peeled back the blanket, revealing her body curled up in a white tank-top and matching cotton panties. Her hair was fanned across her face, a slight smile on her lips. I could've stayed there for hours just staring at her. But my dick had other ideas.

I ran my hand up her back, underneath her top. She sighed and shifted slightly, unfurling her body in response to my touch. I slid my hand around her side and cupped her breast, skimming my thumb over her nipple. She rolled onto her back, opened her eyes, and rewarded me with a lazy smile.

"You're real," I said.

"Good morning to you, too."

I bent my head and kissed her, loving the feel of her flesh in my bed. She moaned against me, wrapping one leg around my waist as I pushed her top up all the way.

"I haven't had morning sex in forever," she purred.

I raised my head from her breast and smiled.

"At your service."

As I explored the landscape with my tongue, she raised her hips, making a slow circle in the air before lowering them to the mattress again. I slid my hand between her legs, feeling her warmth through her panties. I pushed the fabric aside, skimming my finger across her entrance before slipping inside.

She moaned, raising her hips again and pushing herself into my hand. Her arm came up and she tugged at my shirt. I sat up on my heels, pulled off my shirt, then bent over her to remove her panties. I paused, my face between her thighs, to give her a morning kiss.

"Logan," she cried.

"Shhh. You don't want to embarrass yourself in front of my roommates, too, do you?"

She brought my hand up to her face and bit the flesh under my thumb. I grabbed her chin and slid my thumb into her mouth. I coaxed her clit into my mouth as she sucked my thumb, forcing my cock to strain against my boxer briefs. I raised myself up on my elbows and looked at her, my thumb still in her mouth, a look of pure lust in her eyes.

I extracted my hand from her grasp, pulled off my boxers, and climbed on top of her.

"Make it rough," she whispered, sending bolts of electricity through my veins.

Without warning, I flipped her over onto her stomach, slid my arm under her hips, and raised them in the air. Her chest pressed flat against the mattress, I entered her in one quick thrust. She gasped, and then made the most exquisite noise I'd ever heard another human being make.

I rode her hard, my hangover long forgotten. She was whimpering in the mattress, mewling with each thrust. I had never seen this side of Lainey before, and fuck me, I liked it. Her arms were splayed over her head, fisting the blankets as I pumped into her over and over again. I reached around and found her clit, pinching it between my thumb and forefinger.

"Harder," she cried.

I grabbed hold of her hip and rode her for all I was worth. I could feel the orgasm building, from the bottom of my feet, coursing up through my body. I slammed against her as I came, feeling her body react to her own orgasm against mine. My head dropped on her back and we both fell to the bed, exhausted.

She rolled over and peered down at my head, where it rested on her belly.

"Anywhere you have to be right now?" she asked.

"Nope," I said.

*

A little while later, we made it down to the kitchen for breakfast. Or rather, lunch. Lainey sat at the table flipping through the various paperbacks strewn about while I scrambled some eggs and fried the bacon.

"Hey, listen, not that I'm complaining or anything, but what was that all about this morning?" I asked.

She glanced up at me for a moment, then returned to studying the books.

"I wasn't particularly in the mood for sweet and tender after your admission about Brenda Lawson last night."

"Brenda Law—? Oh, shit. Lainey, did that come up?"

"Yup."

I slid the food onto two plates and carried them to the table, putting one down in front of her.

"Listen, about that."

"Two years Logan? Really?"

"Actually, it was closer to three."

"What the fuck?"

"I was lonely. She was broken. It was a disaster waiting to happen."

"Again, for three years?"

I sighed and looked up at the ceiling, wondering if there was any way to explain this to her.

"Bren never left Mountain Valley. She was supposed to go to college in the fall, but in August she found out she was pregnant. Todd Mensky was the father, and she thought they'd get married. He thought differently. His parents sent him off to school as soon as they found out. She stayed here, lived with her parents, and had the baby. Eventually, she got out on her own, but she never met anyone or married.

"We reconnected at a wedding, of all places. I think when she saw me, she saw a chance to erase the past 13 years of her life and start again from high school. I hadn't met anyone, I was getting older...It was just easy."

"And?"

"Well, I really liked her kid. He was twelve, just going through puberty and having a really rough time. He'd never had a male figure in his life, except his grandfather, who was really fucking old. I taught him to play football. It gave him somewhere to divert his anger and frustration with the world."

"And?" she asked again, more insistent this time.

"And I liked the kid more than I liked Bren. What can I say? I was broken, Lain. It took me a couple of years to figure it out, then another to extract myself from the situation. I tried my best to maintain a relationship with the kid, but after a couple of months, Brenda decided to pack up and leave Mountain Valley, really give herself a shot at a new start. It was probably the best decision all around."

"You're the reason she left?"

"Not exactly, but, well, yeah."

She shook her head in disbelief.

"Of all the scenarios I'd envisioned…"

"You'd envisioned scenarios?"

"Stop it," she said, but she didn't look angry.

"You going to be okay?" I asked.

"I'll get over it."

"Are we going to be okay?"

She looked at me and popped the last piece of my bacon into her mouth.

"We'll get over it."

CHAPTER TWENTY-NINE
Lainey

I had known it wasn't going to be easy. It's not like I thought I'd just slide back into his life and we'd pick up where we left off seventeen years earlier. But I hadn't realized how hard it might be. That old hurts like Brenda Lawson might resurface.

I'd dropped Logan off at his workshop a few hours earlier. He showed me around the space and I took a look at some of the designs he was working on. He had his work cut out for him, but he insisted he'd be done in under two months. I told him I'd be back for him around dinner, and took off to explore the city on my own.

My original instinct had been to go down to the Pearl Street Mall and explore the shops and

236

restaurants, but as I approached downtown, I had a change of heart and found myself heading to Central Park. It wasn't too cold a day, and I needed to clear my head.

My first feeling was one of regret that Bella wasn't with me. She'd have loved the wide-open spaces and the steady stream of puppies going by. I missed that dog, never more than when I had something to mull over. And over the past few days, that had been pretty much a constant occurrence.

I found a bench, dusted off the little snow that was there, and took a seat. I pulled out my phone and started dialling. I had business to take care of.

*

The next morning, I looked at Logan across the breakfast table as he buttered his toast. Ethan looked up from his coffee and glanced back and forth between the two of us.

"What's going on?" he asked.

Logan looked up, oblivious.

"What do you mean?" he asked.

"I mean, your woman is looking at you funny," Ethan said.

Steve glanced up from his bowl of sugar

cereal. I ignored them both.

"What are your plans this morning?" I asked Logan.

He shrugged and took a bite of toast.

"I was going to head into the shop. You? Writing?"

"Yeah. I was wondering if you could run an errand with me around two o'clock? I'll come get you."

He looked at me, curious. But he knew better than to ask. If I hadn't offered the information straight away, he wasn't getting it out of me.

"Sure."

I stood up from the table and planted a kiss on his head.

"I'm going to head upstairs and get to work. I'll see you later."

*

I picked Logan up at two, as promised. He was waiting outside for me, already in his coat and scrolling through his phone. I honked and he looked up, smiled, and walked towards the car.

"You going to tell me where we're going?" he asked.

I just smiled and reversed out of the parking lot. He reached forward to turn on the radio and we both rode in silence, listening to Fleetwood Mac go through the most public breakup in history.

"Lain? Why does it look like you're going to the airport?" Logan put down his phone and peered anxiously out the window.

He shifted to check out the backseat.

"You're not leaving, are you?" he asked. "Fuck, Lain, you said we'd work this out."

"I'm not leaving, Logan. Relax."

I pulled into the arrivals pick-up zone, pulling up to the curb. I turned to him.

"You stay here. If someone makes you move, just do a loop and come back. I'll meet you here."

"What the fuck is going on?"

I said nothing but got out of the car. I made my way across the four-lane traffic, feeling like I was in that old Frogger video game. I slipped inside the airport and found the counter I was looking for. I filled out a few papers, and before long, I was exiting the airport, one very happy Bella on the leash by my side.

Logan leapt out of the car and raced towards us. Bella jumped on him, paws on his shoulders as she licked his face enthusiastically. I laughed at the reunion, rubbing Bella's ears as she circled back and forth between the two of us.

"Holy shit, Lain. This is amazing. How long are you planning to stay?"

I opened the back seat and Bella jumped in. I closed the door and looked him in the eye.

"That's the thing. I've been thinking maybe we need to find our own place if we're going to be here for a while."

CHAPTER THIRTY
Six Months Later

I rolled over in bed, the first waves of consciousness passing through my body. I stretched, feeling the warmth from the open window and the slight breeze coming in. There was nothing like August in Mountain Valley. I'd forgotten how good summer could be.

We'd gotten back to town four months earlier, after a highly successful completion of Logan's contract with Damien Axe. The offers were pouring in now, and it was up to Logan to decide which jobs he wanted to accept. Based on some of his choices, I was beginning to think he was more interested in travelling the world than in the work itself.

I agreed to take on two of the re-writes, which kept me busy just long enough to be on set for my production in Mountain Valley. We figured after that was done, we'd head to LA so I could pitch my new film, and if I sold it, I could start writing from wherever Logan's next contract might take us. The story of two teenage lovers who meet up again later in life came easily to me, and Beth was ecstatic about the script. Tess was more than happy to take Bella whenever we left town.

For someone who never wanted to leave their hometown, Logan was getting quite comfortable with the idea of being a global nomad. And for someone who never wanted to return to Mountain Valley, I was getting quite comfortable with the idea of having someplace to call home again.

I cracked open one eye and saw Logan sitting up in bed buck naked, scrolling through his phone. He smiled when he saw me and set the phone aside.

"Good morning," he said.

"Good morning."

I reached over and lazily trailed a hand up his thigh. He grabbed my wrist, pulling my hand away. I pouted.

"No time for that. We've got things to do today."

He jumped out of bed and I groaned. I shut my eyes again and heard the jingling of Bella's collar as she jumped on the bed, followed by sloppy, wet swipes of her tongue across my face.

"Ugh. Morning breath, Bella," I cried.

I pushed her out of the way and got up, heading to the shower. Logan was already inside and I joined him, reaching for the soap and lathering up his back. He stepped away, just out of reach.

"I said, no time for that."

He rinsed off under the spray and stepped out, leaving me alone. What the hell?

"Hey, you know, we've only been living together for four months. I didn't think your sex drive would fall off this quickly," I called.

He opened the shower door and stood there, his cock at full attention.

"Trust me, my sex drive is alive and well. I'm struggling to use my brain here."

I laughed and he shut the door, leaving the bathroom to get dressed.

After a very quick breakfast, the three of us got into the car and Logan started the engine. I didn't bother asking where we were going, figuring if he'd wanted to tell me, he would've. Besides, I'd find out soon enough.

"Have you heard from Desi?" I asked.

"I did. Seems they're having some car trouble. I'm not sure what I was thinking, sending those two out together," Logan mused.

After we'd returned from Boulder, Logan decided to keep Desi on as a full-time employee. She'd learned the business quickly and showed a talent for working with wood, even though she still knew next to nothing. But she'd been playing around in the workshop in Logan's absence and he saw something in her he wanted to nurture.

In the meanwhile, he'd found another job for her. My dad had seen some stuff of Logan's on Instagram he simply had to have, so Desi and Nick Felton, another Mountain Valley local, were driving the stuff out to BC in a moving van. I was curious to know how it was going, as the two of them didn't really seem to hit it off on their departure.

After about twenty minutes, Logan pulled off the main road and I forgot all about Desi and Nick.

"You're taking me back to the B&B?" I asked.

"Grant and Sadie said it's been too long since they've seen you. Besides, I'm done."

"Excuse me?"

"You heard me. I'm done."

Logan had been working on the renovations at the B&B for years. At times, it had been the only thing putting food on his table. It was a total Elgin/Murphy Brown situation and while I was sure he was elated the job was finally complete, I'm sure there were all sorts of feelings going on just then.

"Congratulations," I said softly.

He glanced over at me and smiled.

"You get it."

"I do. I feel the same way every time I hand in a script."

He nodded, clearly able to draw the comparison.

We pulled up outside the large rambling building and Logan killed the engine. We sat there for a moment, surveying the scene in front of us.

"Where it all began," he said.

"Again," I clarified.

"Again."

I leaned over and kissed him.

"Let's go."

We got out of the car and Bella bounded up the walkway to the front door, which flew open to reveal Grant. He had a huge smile on his face and shouted out his greeting as he bent down to pet Bella. When I reached him, I gave him a big hug.

"It's so good to see you, Elena," he said.

"Lainey," I corrected.

Sadie appeared behind him and Bella ran to

her for some love. Sadie was happy to oblige.

"Grant, move aside. Let them in. Come, get in here already."

We all made our way inside and I took a moment to appreciate all the work that Logan had done on the place. The detail was incredible. I knew he was an artist the moment I walked into his shop that first time, but the depth of his talent continued to amaze me.

"Got your room all set up," Sadie said.

I turned around and looked at Logan.

"Our room?" I asked.

"Yup. We're spending the night."

I smiled. I couldn't imagine a better plan. Logan slid his arm around my waist and we went up the stairs. I let him lead me down the hall and he opened the door to the bedroom I'd slept in that first night. There was a small plaque affixed to the door that read, "Wise Matthews Suite." I laughed, delighted.

I walked in and saw a wrapped box on the bed. Glancing at Logan, I walked over and picked it up. Flat and rectangular, I shook it. There were parts. Again, I laughed.

"Chocolates?" I asked.

"Yup."

"You're such a sentimental fool," I said.

I walked around the room, running my hand along the top of the bureau up to the carved, framed mirror. Everything was stunning. I walked over to the bed and sat down, putting my phone on the night table. Something caught my eye and I leaned in. There, carved into the corner of the table was *L+L <3.*

"Or maybe just a fool," I sighed.

"A fool in love," he whispered.

I almost rolled my eyes, but I felt the air in the room change. I glanced over at him and sure enough, he was eyeing me with his patented panty-dropping look. Without even thinking, I started taking off my clothes.

"That's my girl," he said, coming closer and kneeling on the floor at my feet.

He ran his hands up my legs and I sighed, sinking back onto the bed. He crawled between my legs, spreading them apart with his hands as he kissed his way up my thighs.

"I thought we didn't have time for this today," I sighed.

"This morning. Now we're here. We have all the time in the world."

He got to his feet and shed his clothing. I loved watching him pull his shirt over his head, the muscles rippling across his chest and shoulders. I could stare at him for hours. My hand drifted south as he removed his pants. He was definitely ready for me.

"Have you been sporting that thing since the

shower?" I asked.

He looked over at me, saw what I was doing with my hand, and walked over.

"Do you have any idea how much I want you?" he asked.

I trailed my finger back up my belly, circling my nipple before giving it a squeeze.

"Show me," I said.

And he did.

*

A little while later, we were both lying on our backs, staring up at the ceiling and trying to catch our breath.

"Fuck, that was amazing," Logan said.

"I don't think life gets better than this," I agreed.

He turned his head towards mine.

"You don't?" he said.

I'd just blurted it out. I hadn't really thought about it. But now that I had, I realized it was true. Life was pretty damn good. We'd found a way back to each other and we'd figured out how to make it work. How could it get any better? I rolled over on my side to face him.

"No. I really don't. Do you?" I asked.

He smiled and rolled onto his side,

presenting me with the wrapped box from earlier.

"Actually, I think it could get a little better."

I tore my eyes away from the box, raising them to meet his. They were shining, a look of absolute love mixed with terrified uncertainty. I unwrapped the box and lifted the top. I removed the protective sheet, silently noting there was no map included. Before me lay an assortment of chocolates, but in the centre space lay a platinum band with a single, square-cut diamond set in the middle. It was perfect. I raised my eyes once again.

"Are you worried I'm going to say no?" I asked.

"Not really."

"Then why don't you ask me?"

A smile broke out across his face and as he ducked his head a slight blush crept up across his neck. It was so charming I reached out to follow its path with my fingertip. He took my hand in his and kissed it, then took the ring from the box and slid it onto my finger.

"Elena Wise, love of my life, mate of my soul, light at the end of a long, dark, tunnel, please tell me you feel the same. Tell me you want nothing more than to spend the rest of your days with me, discovering the world and each other as we grow old and stay young. Tell me you'll marry me, and accompany me through this crazy adventure of a life we're building. You showed me how to live without the fucking map, Lainey. But I still need you. Say you'll marry me."

I cut him off with a kiss.

"I will."